THE LAST SCION

THE GUARDIANS OF LIGHT: BOOK 1

R. MICHAEL CARD

Gryphon's Gate Publishing

The Last Scion

Copyright © 2017 R. Michael Card

Gryphon's Gate Publishing

550 King St. N.

PO Box 42088 Conestoga

Waterloo, ON.

N2L 6K5

ebook ISBN 978-0-9937651-4-8

Print ISBN 978-0-9937651-8-6

Senia.

Again, her name was whispered on the wind.

She lay awake in darkness. Night deepening beyond her shuttered window. Sleep eluded her, as it had since she'd lain in her straw-stuffed bed that evening, as it had since she had first heard her name called quietly, urgently, barely more than a hushed breath next to her ear.

Come to me, Senia!

She sat up, sweat beading on her brow at the call. This call was much closer, louder, more pressing. She clutched her woolen covers to her neck, the fibers rough against her skin, and searched for any hidden figure. Only three faint lines of moonlight slipped through the slats of the shutters. Her eyes were keen, they always had been, and adjusted well to the black of night, yet she saw no one there. Only her small chest of drawers along the far wall across from her bed and the small night table next to her.

She shivered despite the comfortable warmth of the late spring night.

"Who are you?" she whispered.

Come to me, Senia... please. The call echoed, distant, like the footfalls of someone out on the street below her room, not at all as strong as it had been just a moment before. And there was something in the voice, a strained, hoarse quality as if the last call, so strong and clear, had cost it much.

Senia, terrified, trembling, but somehow curious and drawn, slipped from her bed. Every word, every sound, every breath of this voice resonated within her. She was a bell and it rang through her, beating at her. She couldn't help but move.

She crept to the door of her room, the smooth, worn wooden floor cold against her bare feet.

Her hand touched the latch before she realized she wore only a light linen shift, hanging loosely over her, cut at the knee. She looked over at her chest of drawers.

Senia.

The voice filled her, shook her. Chest forgotten, clothes forgotten, slippers left next to the bed, she slipped into the hall.

She had always been quiet, always able to move undetected. To her own ears, sharper than anyone else she knew, her footfalls were the barest of whispers on the planks of the upper hall. Having lived here since her parents had died, nearly twelve years before, she knew every board and every creak. She was no more than a mouse, scurrying through the corridor, past the rooms of her adopted parents and siblings, down the stairs to the shop and smithy below, and out onto the street.

The village lay still, the sky bursting with stars, the dirt of the road soft with evening moisture against her unshod soles.

It must have been late, for no one else walked the street. No drunks staggering home from The Silver Stag, no late-night lovers. She looked to the wall around the village. Shadows moved slowly along the upper walk, pausing at length to lean on the rough timbres encircling the town. The fact that there were any guards up there at all spoke volumes of the unusual events of the previous day.

Senia, yes, come.

The voice was stronger. She was near. She knew not how she knew where to go, but she did, drawn, inspired.

She crossed the town, unseen, unheard, and found her hand on the latch of the door to The Silver Stag. Without hesitation, she opened the door and slipped inside.

The two large hearths of the tavern glowed faintly, the coals banked for the night. There was only one candle lit, standing in a holder next to the dozing form of Kamdon, the tavern keeper. Forms large and small slept on the long tables, unable to afford a room, or unable to stagger home.

The rough straw, thick over the dirt of the floor, trampled flat by so many, muffled her passing. No more than a shadow, she glided across the large room to the stairs in the back corner.

So close... I have waited so long... you cannot know how long.

She ascended the stairs, a puff of wind, and billowed down the upper hall to a room.

She stopped before the door, her breath still within her, uncertain and yet, completely at ease. There was something familiar about this voice. Was it her father's, from beyond the grave? Maybe an uncle or sibling she had never known. She could not place it, and yet every fiber of her being knew it, responded to it.

"I'm here," she whispered as she entered the room.

It was a simple tavern room, two beds, each with a chest at the foot, a small table under the shuttered window. There was a form on the one bed. In what little moonlight filtered through the closed window, she could make out the sprawled figure of a man. One line of light lit on his cheek, illuminating enough of his face for her to recognize him as the stranger who had staggered into the village late the previous day. He had worn an old cloak over leggings and a shirt, all the same uniform brown. He was young, perhaps only a year or two older than she, and he had carried a large and heavy bundle, something nearly as tall as he, wrapped many times over in rough cloth, which he'd clung to like a lover.

Senia, here.

It wasn't the man who spoke, sleeping still. The voice came from the other bed, from the bundle of rough cloth.

Two strides of her long legs and she was at the bed. Sitting on the lumpy mattress, she reached for the bundle. Her heart raced, pounding within her breast, heaving with gulps of air.

A tentative touch. Her entire body rang like a bell, shuddering.

Take me, take me, I am yours Senia!

Frantic, unable to stop herself, she unwrapped the cloth with trembling hands. Swallowing a lump in her throat as the last shred of wool fell away, she saw that which called to her.

A sword.

But unlike any she had ever seen. The ones her adopted father worked on in the forge were an arm's length of blade, this one was nearly as tall as she. The blade was thick, just wider than the palm of her hand, and sharpened on both sides with a groove running up the center traced with intricate scrollwork. The hilt was made for two large hands with room to spare, at least the length of her forearm, leather wrapped and well worn. The cross-guard and pommel were of thick metal, both delicately carved. The guard depicting roses engulfed in flames and the pommel was fashioned as the head of a hunting cat, proud and stern.

I am Emberthorn and I am yours, Senia.

The trembling in her hand ceased. She caressed the blade, guard, grip, and pommel.

"I... know you," she said shaking her head, for she had never seen such a weapon before. The idea of this being her weapon was ridiculous, for though she was tall for a woman, and stronger than other girls her age from years helping in and around the forge, she would still never be able to lift such a massive weapon let alone wield it. "But... how...?"

The window!

Senia's hand wrapped itself around the smooth leather ridges of the grip as her head tilted. A shutter was opening, a body slinking inside.

Her heart raced for the second time that evening as two eyes, gleaming in the faint light of the moon turned toward her. The figure was covered in black cloth, a mask covering hair and face save for the eyes. A knife appeared in a black-clad hand and a heartbeat later was spiraling through the air.

Time slowed, and in between the pounding beats of her heart, she watched the knife as it tumbled end over end inexorably toward her.

Then a flash, so quick and fierce it pierced time itself.

In the next moment, Senia found herself standing, the knife embedded deeply in the door to the room, Emberthorn held easily in her small, fine hands. How easily it had moved, so quickly, knocking the knife from the air.

The landing of the knife woke the man in bed.

For the next set of heartbeats, the room was silent and still as the assassin, girl, and man each absorbed the impossible made real.

You see, I was meant for you, Emberthorn said, the words echoing in her head accompanied by what sounded like purring.

The man in the bed was up in a heartbeat and a swift high kick sent the still stunned assassin tumbling back out of the window. He turned to her then.

"Who are...?"

"Behind you," she cut him off as another form filled the window.

The man spun another kick, his foot captured by the attacker in black. The assailant threw the foot up and away, but the man simply flipped himself around with it, landing on the same foot before launching himself bodily at the man in the window, both disappearing down out of sight.

Follow!

And without thinking, she did.

Light, quick steps, a hop to the table below the window, then out in the night air. Emberthorn moved with her, as one. Flashing out to the side as she tucked around, spinning forward, then reversing in her grip as she righted. She thrust downward, slicing into the ground, and somehow this slowed her, so she touched down lightly.

Exhilarated, blood rising, her hair wild around her as it settled, she plucked the sword from the ground, and spun it upright, stalking toward the fight already under way.

The stranger from the room above, though he had no weapon, fought like nothing she had ever seen before. He kept at bay seven men in black though they carried knives and swords and he had but his bare palms. One other dark figure lay splayed awkwardly in the dirt.

Battle! Emberthorn cried, filling her with ecstasy.

A stroke, wide and smooth, and two men were down.

The others backed away quickly, terror in their eyes.

"I am whole again. Feel my wrath." The words were Emerthorn's, but it had been her lips that had whispered them.

No! She screamed at the blood-lusted blade. But though she could feel, could think, could understand the death she had caused, she wasn't in control.

The stranger tackled one of the attackers, hands deftly redirecting the assassin's knife, before springing away lightly to land on the other side. The knife embedded in the assailant's black-clad chest.

From eight to four, the attackers' numbers had dropped too quickly. They fled.

Like nothing more than the darts her father threw at the board in his forge, Senia released Emberthorn in a side-long toss. The blade turned as it spun and cut down two more of the fleeing forms before spinning impossibly back to her hands.

"I am alive again!" She bellowed his words, feeling only its rush of exhilaration.

Emberthorn, please! Stop.

What?

I want my body back, I... please... release me.

Oh! Right... Sorry.

She fell to her knees on the soft earth of the street, weeping, stomach churning at the easy violence she had committed.

CHAPTER 2

*A*hrn contemplated the two last fleeing assailants, but they were already at the wall, mage-stim enhanced limbs propelling them up to the walk, then over into darkness.

Breathing heavy, he turned to the crumpled form of the girl kneeling in the dirt, the artifact-sword Emberthorn still clutched in one hand.

An incongruous image next to the enraptured beauty who brought swift death to The Blacklord's men.

So, this was what a Scion looked like.

All his life he had been taught that no Scions remained. The Blacklord's men had hunted down every man, woman, and child who possessed any trace of the blood of The Guardians. Apparently, the monks at the abbey and The Blacklord's men had all been wrong.

He tilted his head as he contemplated her in the silent starlight. Long, unbound hair, covering her face and shoulders. It was hard to tell the color in such dimness, but he guessed it was amber, soft red-brown. A moment before, as she had fought impassioned, she had seemed a spirit, or perhaps a statue of the Goddess Aehryn, First of the Gods, come to life. A fleeting thought had swept through his mind, of her as an Avatar of The Vanished God Herself. Arms fine yet strong, legs long and slender, she was tall for a girl, nearly as tall as he, who stood above half the men he knew.

No, she was no God, but she must be a Scion. Beyond her perfect form, there was the way she had wielded Emberthorn. The massive mystic sword was over-heavy for a weapon of its size, few mortal men could lift it let alone attempt to strike with it. The blade would only allow itself to be held, and with ease, by a true-blooded descendant of the Guardians.

He took a step toward her. His soft tread on the earth no more than a whisper, but in the silence of the moment, it startled her. She flinched, rising suddenly, sword held like nothing more than a twig in one outstretched hand. With its amazing length and her extended arm, it came up a hair from his chin.

He stopped, head tilting back.

He retreated a step, raising his hands. "I am no threat to you."

Her face was still mostly hidden behind a veil, floating wisps of hair, but he could see her eyes. Azure pools, wide and deep, enveloping him with their intensity.

"Who are you?" she asked hesitantly, hoarse from weeping.

He smiled. "I'm Ahrn. May I ask your name?"

The radiant pools dimmed with a squint. She didn't trust him. He couldn't blame her. She didn't know him.

"I'm a monk of Embreth the Keeper. I will not harm you. That sword was in my care, but it would seem that is no longer the case. It called to you didn't it?"

Her head turned away slightly as she closed off those beautiful eyes even more. "How did you know?"

"A lucky guess. I have been taught since I was a boy that such artifacts are very rare and special. There are... only a few who might wield it, and to them, it would rage like thunder until they were bonded."

"Bonded?"

"As you are now. The sword to you and you to it."

"What does that mean?" She hadn't let down the sword, and though he had moved back a pace, it quivered in the air before him, expectant.

He steadied himself. "I would be happy to explain to you, but perhaps not here? Perhaps somewhere more comfortable?"

"Here is fine."

"Here is fine," he repeated as sweat blossomed on his brow. He had no desire to anger a Scion. "Bonding is when a Scion, such as yourself, and an artifact of power, such as Emberthorn, join to become one, their thoughts together, their powers multiplied by the joining."

"How did you know that name... Emberthorn? Does it speak to you too?"

"No, but the monks have studied such artifacts for hundreds of years. There are a limited number, and each has a name and certain powers."

"Oh." The tip of the blade sank, slowly. "What did you call me?"

"When?"

"Just now, you said I was a SIGH-ON?"

Was it possible she didn't know what she was? "A Scion yes. A true descendant of one of the Guardians from the Lost Age."

Her mouth and eyes tightened. "A what from when?"

It would definitely appear as though she had no inkling of her heritage. He sighed. "This is going to take a while to explain."

"I'm not tired."

"No, the sword will be sustaining you. You won't tire like the rest of us, not anymore."

The razor point of Emberthorn rose again. "You keep talking like that! What are you saying?"

"Very simply, I'm saying that from this moment onward, your life will be... already is... changed. You are a Guardian now, and men will fear or revere you."

Now the sword did drop, easily cutting a trough in the dirt of the road, as her shoulders slumped.

Her voice was small, soft, "I didn't want this."

"From what I've heard, once you and the sword were close enough, it wouldn't matter what you had wanted before. It is destiny. This is who you are."

"I'm Senia, a smith's daughter. I'm..." the words fled, caught by a lost wind.

"A Scion."

"A Scion? I don't even know..."

"I can help you." He wanted to. Wanted to be close to

this wondrous woman, to sink into the oceans of her eyes. He wanted to know the scent of her hair, the feel of her embrace. He wanted...

He snapped himself from the thought, roughly. Such were not the thoughts of a monk of Embreth, devoted to knowledge, to secrets, not to such longings of the flesh. He told himself it was only the fascination of her being a Scion. The lie soothed him.

She swept the loose hair away from her face, tucking it behind a perfectly formed ear. Her eyes, lost lakes of blue rimmed with tears, turned to him. Then, like lightning, blinding and wondrous, and swifter than the eye could follow, she threw herself on him, arms around him, hot tears on his shoulder. Somehow, all this managed so swiftly and with perfect grace, despite the six-foot sword still held firmly in her left hand.

His arms were around her before he knew what he was doing... and when he did know... he didn't stop.

"Help me." Hot breath warmed his neck. A shiver ran through him, his entire body responding to the call.

He held her closer.

"I will."

A thought struck him then, a foretelling perhaps. Certain that hers would not be the only life forever altered this night.

CHAPTER 3

*S*enia sat cross-legged on the lumpy mattress in Ahrn's small room, facing where he sat on his bed. She wasn't looking at him though. Her head down, she watched her fingers trace the intricate whorls and images carved over Emberthorn's hilt and blade. She felt the minute ridges of each rune in the cold metal, her touch so receptive, sending chills down her spine.

Emberthorn was purring again. He hadn't said much since the fight. He seemed to have mixed feelings about Ahrn. On the one hand, Ahrn was the one who had brought him to her and had taken good care of him in the meantime, but on the other hand, Ahrn and his monk friends had kept Emberthorn locked away in a chest deep beneath their abbey for years, no place for such a regal and amazing weapon to be.

Senia agreed. Emberthorn was the most marvelous thing she had ever seen.

"Are you ready?" Ahrn asked, settled. No candle had

been lit. Now, even more than before, darkness was no hindrance to her sight, and Ahrn didn't need light to talk.

"I don't know." She dragged each word out. She needed to know more about Emberthorn and what meeting him meant for her, but so much other uncertainty floated around her. Did she really want it to land?

"When you are, let me know."

A long silence. Even the crickets were hushed this night.

Her thoughts whirled and warred within her. She had to know, but what would that mean? He had said her life was changed. She knew it was true, but by how much, and how far would it go? Where would it take her? What of her family? Her emotions stormed, combining or flashing apart with each heartbeat. She wanted to be a simple girl and a great warrior. She knew both were not possible together. One life would win. One element of her lost.

Finally, she sighed. "Tell me." She looked up at him then, her hair had fallen over her face. She let it hang, loose and faintly floating in the breeze from the window. Even though she no longer watched, her fingers kept tracing patterns on the blade, she knew each engraving now, as she knew her own body.

"Long ago, in the time of beginning, the world was simple. There was no magic. It is said the people worshiped nature, finding spirits in all things. They didn't know the gods then."

"What has this to do with me? I know the tale of the coming of the Gods, the rise and fall of Magic, the Death of Aehryn. I have heard the Priests speak on holy days."

Her emotions strung tight, she drew back her sharp tongue, halting further words.

He seemed lost for a moment. It was amazing how clearly she could see the confusion, the lines on his face, his light brown eyes searching. He was trying to help her, and she wasn't being very civil about it.

"I'm sorry," she said softly, "Please go on."

He grinned, his wide mouth spreading to crease his cheeks. She smiled with him, her heart eased.

"Well, perhaps there are some parts of the Tale of Aehryn your priest has not mentioned. Perhaps he told you of the First Coming of Aehryn of All Things, and how she brought magic with her, then encouraged the other gods to follow suit and gift men with their own individual blessing of power. How men over the following centuries came to abuse those powers. How Aehryn returned as a mortal woman and gathered followers to strike down the oppressors and tyrants who used magic for their own gain. But did he ever mention how those followers, mostly simple men and women with no magic, had the power to strike down Wizards of great power?"

Senia tilted her head, looking away. The priest in her village was well-studied and learned. He had mentioned something once, though it refused to return to her memory.

She shook her head.

Ahrn pointed at Emberthorn. "That is how."

It was a most glorious battle, the blade sighed wistfully.

"Oh."

"It was in that battle when the Arch-Wizard Nacryssan

arrived with his legions of undead and all seemed lost, that Aehryn sacrificed herself, taking with her all the magic of the Gods."

Senia nodded. Everyone knew of Aehryn's Sacrifice, giving up her immortal Godhood and vanishing into the Void, taking the power of the great Magics. She wasn't able to take all the magic, for men had lived with the power for so long that some magic had soaked into bones and sinews. The Wizards of today were spare and weak compared to those of ancient times.

Ahrn Continued. "Those whom Aehryn had gifted with weapons such as Emberthorn were all that remained. They were the Guardians of her will, ensuring that those with magic or any other significant power over other men did not abuse it."

"Why would Cleric Donolan not mention these people?" Yet that wasn't the only question whirling in her mind. "And where are these Guardians now? What happened to them?"

"There is only so much we know today. These battles took place long ago, and your Priest, through divine connection with his God, may know much of that time, but what came after was of little concern to the remaining Gods. They distanced themselves from men, who had abused the powers the Gods had given. The Guardians lived in a time we call The Lost Age, where few records are kept and even the Gods keep their knowledge from their Priests."

Why would a God keep secrets from their followers? She asked Ahrn as much.

In the gloom, Ahrn grimaced, which sunk into a frown. "They are afraid."

"They are Gods. What could they fear?"

"In that Age of Power, some of the Arch-Wizards were so great in their ability that they came close to rivaling the Gods themselves. Add to this the knowledge that a God can die, as Aehryn showed us all, and imagine how they must have felt. Once all powerful, now vulnerable. They feared too much knowledge given to man might be like too much magic."

Senia nodded. Then a final question came to her. Her gaze, so clear in the darkness, sought Ahrn's full, dark eyes. "How do you know all this?"

"I'm a monk of Embreth, the Keeper of knowledge and Secrets. She among all the Gods chooses her followers carefully, searching their souls for purity so that she might share her secrets with them. She fears us not, for as we know her secrets, she knows ours."

A slow shiver trembled down Senia's spine. What would it be like to have someone know you so intimately?

Like I do?

Her heart froze.

You need not fear my oneness with you. This is how it should be. Plus, you are the only one who can hear me, so who would I tell?

Senia was little relieved.

Don't you trust me?

Of course she did. How could she not? Emberthorn was family... more than family... twin, a part of her as she was of him. Yet where had that familiarity come from?

As if speaking to both of them, Ahrn returned to his story, "You are a descendant of one of those Guardians. One of your ancestors once wielded Emberthorn, fighting at the side of Aehryn The Mortal and tending to the world after Her Vanishing."

Senia tilted her head, looking away, questions bubbling up within her. "But, if that is so, wouldn't I know? It's true, I never knew much of my true parents. They died when I was still very young, but wouldn't they have possessed the sword? Shouldn't it have been passed down to them?"

"The Age of Power lasted many hundreds of years before the Lost Age came. The Guardians would have had many children, yet only one could have inherited the Aehryn-Gift. Somewhere in the mists of history, your family line broke off from the one that took the blade. You have the blood, but even your great-great-grandparents might never have known they were related to a Guardian."

This only left her with more questions, one foremost among them: "You never answered my question. What happened to the Guardians?"

"The War of the Guardians. They had done such a good job rooting out evil and corruption that men started to fear them. With their artifacts, they were now the ones with great power over others. People demanded that the Guardians lay down their Aehryn-Gifts and use them no more. To a Guardian, this was nearly unthinkable. So, men fought against the Guardians and Guardians against men."

Emberthorn's mood shifted at the mention of the war. *Did they not know we were there to protect them!*

"Eventually, most of the Guardians, though it was like losing a limb, gave up their items, for they could not fault these men, who were innocent and misguided. Other Guardians fought back, unable to give up a part of themselves. These were changed by the carnage they leveled on humanity. In the end, their artifacts abandoned them, for their souls were no longer pure. They died from the loss."

Ravedon gave me up willingly, Emberthorn commented, *I could still feel him until the day he passed. He was a great man, a pure man, as you are pure Senia.*

A tear beaded in her eye, then released, tracing a stream down her cheek to the crook of her mouth, where she wiped it away. So much tragedy and death. So meaningless.

I'm sorry, Emberthorn said, voice heavy, *I think that was my tear.*

Indeed, now that she was becoming more aware of their connection she could feel that though Ahrn's story had struck a chord within her, it was the sword's sorrow which she felt above all else.

"Over time," Ahrn went on. "The Guardians died off. Many had children who would have inherited their artifacts, but the bonding, the physical touch of the magical item, never happened. Many forgot their heritage."

Ahrn paused, drawing a steadying breath. "Until The Blacklord came."

Senia knew of The Blacklord, but only as a fairy-tale, an empty warning parents used to garner obedience. He lived in some land far to the east, covered in black clouds, practicing dark magic, but he was no real threat here.

"Though his true name is lost to us, this man, with a strain of wizard's blood, discovered tomes of dark magic and with those built his power until few could defeat him. He feared only one thing. The rise of new Guardians. So, he sent his men out into all the lands on a two-fold mission. First was to find the artifacts and bring them to him so no Guardian might use any against him. Second was to seek the Scions, the descendants of the guardians, and kill them all.

"Those men tonight were The Blacklord's assassins." He paused, drawing a long breath before he went on. "The Monks of the Abbey of St. Panris, where I lived, had but the one artifact. Our Abbey is very old and in disrepair. We were taking Emberthorn to St. Antin Abbey, our great stronghold, when The Blacklord's men found us. The other monks..." Ahrn's voice faltered. She looked to see his lips purse as he swallowed some dark memory. "...They kept the assassins at bay while I escaped with the sword. I fled for two days before finding this village. I had thought I'd lost them, but..."

Senia's thoughts rushed and raged once again. She filled in what he wasn't saying.

"Now they know I'm a Scion."

He nodded. "I'm sorry. I have endangered you and your family."

And within the span of her next heartbeat, everything crashed into place around her, a wall of thoughts and connections which led to only one place. A place she did not want to go, an unknown.

Emberthorn's strong voice called to her. *You need not be*

afraid. A Guardian is a Force of Aehryn, of truth, justice, and righteousness. These men of The Blacklord are nothing. Can you not see what you are meant for? You, Senia, can fight... and with me... you can win.

She listened, hollow. 'Senia' could that really be her name anymore? Was she still the girl she had been before she'd gone to bed that evening? She knew now she couldn't stay. More than this, her family too would have to flee, all because of her actions... and she couldn't go with them. Would they understand? Could they ever understand how her life had been shattered?

So many questions tore at her soul, a whirlwind of pain and loss.

She looked down at Emberthorn, but the sword was silent on the topic.

"Senia?"

Lost in her own turmoil, she looked up through her curtain of hair. "Yes." Was that her voice, so soft and weak?

"I'm here if you need anything." He hesitated, more yet unsaid.

"Where can they go?"

He must have understood she spoke of her family. "To the west and south. The Blacklord's spies are everywhere, and he watches us monks as keenly as we watch him. If they go on their own, keeping hidden and can get past the Silver Mountains to the lands of the Jhin Dynasty then they should be safe enough." He paused again before asking, "You are adopted yes?"

"How did you know?"

"You said something earlier about your 'true parents',

that and an artifact will always call to the first of a blood-line. If you have a family, and it did not call to one of your parents, then..."

She nodded.

He rose. "This is good." He moved softly, swiftly across the floor to her as he spoke. "If they don't share your blood, it will be that much harder for The Blacklord to track them. He will come for you, do not doubt that, but he will eventually lose interest in a family that has no Scion blood." He knelt before her, eyes pleading, seeking, dark and warm.

"Can you promise they will be safe?" She reached out to him.

Both his hands enveloped hers, his palms hard and warm. "I can promise nothing, I'm sorry. This would be their best chance, of that I'm certain."

Senia looked away.

He spoke softly as she considered. "I can guarantee you this. If you stay, or if you go with them, The Blacklord will come at you with all the power he possesses. With Emberthorn, you may be able to defend yourself, but you won't be able to protect them all, not forever."

This she knew. "Then let us get them gone with all haste and be away from here ourselves." The words were ash in her mouth, vile and choking.

CHAPTER 4

*C*ascading color, from deepest purple to flashing orange washed across the clouds of dawn. The sun was not yet up, but light was filtering in around them. It was a beautiful scene, though Ahrn could enjoy little of it, watching, from a distance the tearful final embraces between Senia and her family.

They were in a loose grove of trees not far from her village near where the western road split. Her family would follow the western road toward the Silver Mountains, Ahrn and Senia would follow the north road to the kingdom of Hallania, and the Abbey of St. Antin.

It was later than Ahrn would have liked when Senia finally came to him, the sun had risen fully above the horizon, but despite his impatience, he couldn't fault her. He hadn't known his family, raised as a boy in the Abbey, but he had imagined a family for himself many times and could imagine the pain of having to leave them, forever.

Senia pulled Emberthorn from where she had struck it into the ground then walked past Ahrn, stern, tall, and silent.

Her stride was long, and he rushed to catch her, matching it.

They walked all morning in silence.

Ahrn had bought supplies for the trip as Senia had convinced her family to leave then helped them pack their life away. They ate a sparse lunch of fresh bread, sharp cheese, and new berries, and still she didn't speak.

It was only as the afternoon wore on, many miles behind them that she turned to him as they walked.

"Do you have a family?" she asked, her tone held the hint of an edge. She was still freshly stung by her emotions.

He shook his head. "If I did, I never knew them. I was given to the Abbey as a young boy. I sometimes have flashes of a face, a young woman: kind, with light hair and brown eyes. Perhaps my mother or an aunt, or perhaps of no relation at all. I don't know. The Monks were my family and all I knew for as long as I can remember. Now they are..." He swallowed hard. He didn't know if any had survived the attack on their caravan. He hoped that some might be still alive, traveling onward to St. Antin. He could only hope.

Senia looked away. "I'm sorry, I forgot."

Silence stretched, like the dusty road before them.

After a long moment, she said, "it would seem we have both lost much."

He smiled, hoping to lift her spirits. "You have also gained something very special, Senia."

She looked askance at him, disbelieving.

"Emberthorn is a very special blade, an artifact of great power and magic."

She shrugged. "What do I know of magic? What do I need with magic? I'm just a girl!" Her voice grew sharper, each word laced with confusion and resentment.

Ahrn made sure he spoke in soft tones, light and easy. "Emberthorn is of spirit, and Aehryn-gifts of spirit are considered some of the most powerful, the most precious."

He received another sidelong look from Senia, but this one with a hint of curiosity. "Truly?"

He nodded. It was the truth, he would not deceive her.

She looked away suddenly, rolling her eyes and muttered, "I don't want to talk to you right now."

"My apologies then," Ahrn said softly.

"What? Oh, not you, I was talking to Emberthorn. He keeps trying to help, but our connection is so close he ends up throwing too much at me at once. It's nice to talk normally... with you. Please, keep going." Her voice was soft now. He could hear the sorrow edging through, her soul still tender as any open wound.

"I will tell you what I know of magic, how's that?" he said with a smile.

She nodded for him to go on.

"Imagine a star with eight points, four larger, longer points at the top, bottom, and to the sides, with lesser points on each diagonal. This is the cycle of energies and elements which make up the world. At the top is spirit and it is linked to the element of fire. Spirit is what connects all things together it is the energy of life. As I said, some consider it to be highest of the Prime Domains."

"What's a domain?"

"Just an area of magic, a specific type of power. Usually a wizard or a scion-artifact can use only one domain, one area of magic. There are some rare wizards who can use two domains. These are called Dual-Talents. Even rarer are those who can use three or all four of the Prime Domains, called Multitalents."

"Is that what the Blacklord is?"

"Yes, a true and powerful multitalent."

She shuddered.

He moved on. "Spirit is at the top and directly across from it, at the bottom, is the domain of body, which is linked to the element of earth. Each point on the star sits across from its opposite, that which is most in contrast to it. Where spirit is ethereal and energy, body is solid and material. Have you heard of the Daughters of Ehlani?"

"The healers?"

"Yes. Not all of them have magic, but some do. Such healers would be earth-talents, able to fix and heal a person's body." Senia nodded. He went on. "The two points on the sides are also opposites. On the left side is the domain of soul, linked to the element of water, and on the right side is the domain of mind, linked to the element of air and wind."

"Sorry, what was that? I'm getting a little confused."

Ahrn thought of how to explain this a little clearer. An idea came to him. "Think of a compass."

"A compass?"

"Yes, where spirit is north, mind is east, body is south, and soul is west. Does that make sense?"

She nodded. "I think so."

He continued, excited. "And each domain has a companion element, in the same order, they would be: fire, wind, earth, and water.

She nodded. "Got it, but..."

"But?"

"I feel like I should know this, but what is the difference between spirit and soul?"

Ahrn laughed lightly. "That's a fair question. I guess I'm used to these terms, but for anyone else, it might be hard to see the difference." He thought a moment before going on. "The easiest way to explain it is that spirit is the force which creates everything and connects all things to each other. It is larger than one person, it is the essence of all life. Soul is what feels, it is the seat of our emotions, the individual and unique core of our being. It is our heart. Does that make sense?"

"So, Spirit is everywhere and felt by all things, but soul is personal, what creates our emotions?"

"Roughly, yes."

"I see."

"So, Spirit, Mind, Body, and Soul are the four Prime Domains. Then there are four Lesser Domains."

She gave a short laugh. "There's more?"

"Yes, do you want me to stop for now?"

"No, it's fine, go on."

"I'll try to be as clear as I can. If you think of that

compass again, between spirit and mind, so northeast, is the domain of destruction, linked to the sub-element of storm."

Senia nodded with a bit of a laugh. "Destruction and storm, good." She was smiling now. She seemed to be taking this lesson as some sort of memory game, distracted from her worries for the moment. "Thank you for going through this slowly, Emberthorn tried to jam this all into my head earlier and it just seemed a jumble of meaning-less stuff."

"We'll see if you're still willing to thank me when I'm done," he said lightly, then continued taking his time. "Between mind and body, so southeast, is the domain of deception, which is linked to the sub-element of darkness or shadow."

"That one doesn't sound so nice."

"Magic is what it is and it's not always nice."

She took a moment then nodded, seeming to accept that explanation, so he went on. "Between body and soul, to the southwest, is the domain of creation, linked to the sub-element of growth and life. And finally, between soul and spirit, so northwest, is the domain of truth and the sub-element of light."

She sighed. "That is a lot to take in."

"Luckily all you need to worry about is Spirit for now. Emberthorn's spirit is very strong, and yours is as well if I had my guess." He could sense... something from her, a pull to a place deep within him. Those with power over spirit had the ability to inspire others, rouse them to one purpose or another. She was still fresh in her powers, but already he felt drawn to her.

"I can't imagine what you are going through," he said, placing a hand on her shoulder reassuringly, giving a soft squeeze. "But even I, with no magic to speak of, can sense the strength of your spirit Senia. You're connected to all things, more-so than any other person. Your family will always be with you through that connection."

She was quiet for a long time as they walked. His hand fell to his side again, hoping he had helped to ease her mood, at least a little.

"I can sense them," she said finally. "My family. Emberthorn has taught me how to find them, to feel them. You're right, I'll always have this connection." Her voice was getting choked up by the time she finished, not with sorrow but a newfound hope.

After another long moment, she said simply, "Thank you." Her free hand—for her left still clung to Emberthorn, held in a reversed grip so the blade flashed in the sun behind her—sought his. Soft flesh of long fingers traced across his palm, curling around to hold his hand, as he too gripped hers. Warmth flooded through him, though the day was already hot. The pull he felt from her surged. Perhaps the contact of their skin had connected their spirits in some way he could not fathom. Looking to her, as she turned to him, he fell into the depths of her eyes, sparkling as the sun on water. While still entranced by her eyes he noticed her soft, pink lips part slightly.

He began to lean in, bringing his lips to hers but stopped himself, barely into the movement.

He had vows to uphold. Vows of purity and chastity he couldn't ignore.

He squeezed her hand, hoping to reassure her then drew back, smiling faintly, hoping to cover his weakness. This contact, and only this, would be what he was allowed. No matter how strongly her spirit called to his.

CHAPTER 5

*S*enia stood her ground.

It was late in their second day out, and they had found a village in which they hoped to find some food or supplies. What they found instead was a local tyrant. Rather he'd found them.

"I said, give me the sword, girly!" In his froth of irritation, spittle flew from the man's lips as he spoke.

This man needs to be taught a stern lesson, Emberthorn said evenly, belying the hum of energy and anticipation surging into Senia from the sword.

The man before her was large, taller than her by a head, thick and meaty in limb and body. Small eyes in a round red face flared with annoyance. His snarl revealed a patchwork of rotting teeth behind fleshy lips. He loomed over her, leaning in, massive arms out to the side, seeking to intimidate.

It was very clear that this man lived to create fear—if the rest of the small village huddling behind him wasn't enough evidence, his every twitch and pace exuded threat, violence, and raw physical power. He could deliver too; he wasn't all bluster. He could move very quickly for one so large. Ahrn, groaning, flat on his back beside her could attest to that.

Senia met the man's gaze passively. "No."

He swung.

She crouched, ducking under the blow with a wide step back, strong and steady. Emberthorn flew out to the side, her right hand joining her left on the hilt in a reversed grip. The blade flashed as her hands flew to her right shoulder. With her wider stance and greater distance from the man, the blade skimmed over his flesh, drawing a fine bloody line from hip to opposite shoulder, shredding his shirt in the process.

The man reared back with a feral scream. Chances are he didn't know the touch of pain, only how to inflict it.

She stood slowly from her wide low stance, keeping her distance.

"That was a warning."

You don't know how good that felt, Emberthorn sung with glee. *It's been ages since I've smote a tyrant, even if he is the tyrant of a tiny village.*

Senia smiled, feeling the sword's euphoria. She had no idea what it felt like to smite a tyrant, or at least she hadn't, until now. She had to admit, it felt good.

The man planted a hot, furious gaze upon her.

"No one strikes me!"

A flash, across and down, faster than her eye could

follow, though her hands knew exactly what they were doing.

The man's shirt fell away. A second thin, bloody line marked him, shoulder to hip, creating an 'X' across his torso.

"Second warning. You don't get a third."

Dazed, in pain, rage fading, the man's brows lowered, his beady eyes shrinking in suspicion.

"What are you?"

"I am a Scion, Guardian of the weak."

Give him a Mark of Justice!

A what?

A Mark of... Oh, never mind I'll do it.

Her right hand, releasing the blade became suddenly, intensely hot. With incredible speed, she stepped in and placed her hand on the man's chest. There was a searing and sizzling sound. The man cried out. She stepped back, hand cold.

The man's eyes flashed wide as a hand came up to the hand-shaped burn, touching and flinching away.

"What?"

"That is a Mark of Justice." Emberthorn was speaking through her, she listened, intrigued to learn of this new ability. "Leave this village and never return. If you do, the righteous fire of my wrath will consume you. If you threaten or willfully harm another, or break the Gods' Law in any other way, for the rest of your days, Holy fire will take you. Do you understand?"

The man, face slack, eyes frozen with terror, nodded, dumb.

"Now go," Senia said, back in control as Emberthorn retreated back to the blade.

He bobbed his head again, cheeks flapping, then spun, sprinting from the village.

Ahrn got to his feet carefully, still unsteady.

"That was amazing." He was shaking his head, trying to clear it. A dark spot forming on his chin, soon to be a bruise. "What exactly was that?"

"If you heard what I said, then you know as much as I do."

"Emberthorn's doing?"

"Yes."

"Impressive."

The villagers drew closer, forming a circle around Senia and Ahrn, though maintaining a distance of a few paces, bowing and whispering thanks.

One particularly brave woman stepped forward, small and round, wearing a tattered dress and thick apron.

"Great Lady," she said, voice reverent, bowing. "We have no common house here, but if you wish, you may stay in my house tonight, dine at my table. It would be an honor."

Senia looked to Ahrn, who shrugged. She gauged the placement of the sun and looked back to the woman.

"Thank you for your offer, I'm humbled by it. However, we have far to go, and there is still much time today for travel. If you have some food we might take with us, we would be grateful for it. Only if you have extra though."

The woman nodded. "With Osdak gone, the stores in

his silos and barns will keep us well through to the next harvest. We can afford to give some. Come, this way."

A short while later they were on the road again, packs stuffed with dried meats and fruits and two fresh loaves of bread.

Ahrn, every few hundred feet along, would take a heavy breath and let out a long sigh, shaking his head.

After one too many of these, Senia put a hand on his shoulder, stopping him. "What is it?"

He raised his brow, his eyes distant. "What?"

"Something is bothering you."

His head tilted slightly. "Is this a new Scion power, reading minds?"

She smiled. "I can see you're distracted, no powers needed."

"Oh." He looked away and drew in another long breath. This time he let it out in several short laughs, still shaking his head. "It's just..." His eyes came to hers again, soft, brown, honest. He simply looked at her for some time before going on. "No one has beaten me, not like that, not that quickly. It's been years since anyone has been able to lay me low with a single punch."

"Oh." Now she understood. "I see."

His expression darkened. "Are you mocking me?"

Her smile faded. "No. I have seen you fight when it matters, and there is nothing there to mock. You are a skilled warrior."

He turned away. "Then why couldn't I handle one large man?" He muttered something after this, something about "Master... would be..."

"Master who would be what?" she asked, continuing to walk.

A sigh. "Master Elia would be disappointed."

"Who is Master Elia?"

"The woman who taught me to fight."

"A woman, truly?" She tilted her head to see him better.

A grimace. "Truly. When I was a boy, she was twice my size and terrified me. She had a certain scowl and with her iron gray hair seemed more some spirit of rock and fury. Then I grew up and stood over her by a full head and shoulders, still she scared the life out of me. She was a hard woman. Even when I was bigger than her, she crashed me to the ground more times than I care to recall. She is... was?" He looked away for a moment. "She is the best warrior I have ever known. She must have survived."

"Were there many woman monks?" Senia found a bubbling sense of curiosity within her. She wasn't sure why this was so important to her at the moment, but she needed to know.

He nodded. "Embreth accepts all, unlike some of the other orders."

"Oh." Her stomach churned. She couldn't understand her feelings, didn't know why the thought of other women around Ahrn upset her, but it did.

"You must remember," he went on, "that Embreth is the God of Knowledge and Secrets. We were taught about the biology of animals and humans early on. We knew of all the differences between men and women to dispel any myths or silliness that might arise." He gave her a coy half grin before he went on. "I know all about how your body works."

Heat rushed to her face, and to many other places she didn't want to think about, but which apparently, he knew quite well. That thought only caused more heat to flood her.

His smile faded, and he looked away again. "That's why the monks of Embreth are some of the best healers, next only to the Daughter of Ehlani." As his gaze had moved away, so had it taken some of the intense warmth within her. She tried to calm her suddenly racing heart with the thought that if anything were to happen to her, he would be there to tend to her.

But would you want him to tend to you, I wonder? Emberthorn cut into her thoughts. *I suppose it would depend on where the wound was, wouldn't it?*

More heat flooded through her, trembling within her, twisting her stomach.

Emberthorn sighed. *Sometimes I forget how young you are, my dear. I am sorry for the jest.*

A sense of peace seeped into her hand holding the sword and slowly, as with one great peaceful exhalation, she calmed.

In truth, she didn't know much about this man, who she had been traveling with for nearly two days. Perhaps it was time to learn.

"What was it like there?"

"At the abbey?"

She nodded.

"Majestic." His eyes were distant with memory, then he

laughed. "And old. On the edge of a plateau with mountains like a blanket around us. It was on the southern fringe of the kingdom of Sandria, the Navrin Mountains, which marked the border, rising up south of us. There were two ridges stretching down out of the mountains, one to the east and one to the west. We were at the north end of the plateau, a river rushing by just outside the walls, becoming a beautiful waterfall where the highlands ended.

"I can remember many a night, sitting outside the abbey, watching the spray of the water, hearing the crash far below, and thinking there was no more majestic sight in the world." He turned toward her then, mouth open to say something, but then he blinked and shook his head, looking back down the road ahead.

Then another short laugh. "Everything around us was majestic and striking, except the abbey. It was old, walls crumbled in places, patched with wood. It had once been the castle of some warlord, in ages gone by. We were few, we had no stonemasons among us, mostly farmers or miners from the few villages that clustered near the river where it continued in the valley below. We didn't know how to keep up such things. It would have taken a lot of work, I think. By the time I arrived, it was probably already past saving. In the sixteen years I was there it just went from bad to worse, walls I'd stood on as a child, that had seemed sturdy, were long gone when we left."

"Did you like it there?" Senia asked, piecing together the images he provided, weaving a tapestry in her mind's eye.

"By the time I was old enough to decide what I liked and what I didn't, I hadn't known anything else. I liked the feel of the place, the history, knowing that once, powerful men had lived here, perhaps controlled much of the country around them. I didn't like the drafts. It was a bit warmer in the south than here, but as high as we were, there were great cold winds that would come down out of the mountains, blasting through the many holes in whatever room you found yourself. In winter, we got little snow, but the winds were a constant thing, howling through the abbey sucking the heat from your bones." Despite the rough description he smiled, wide mouth creasing his cheeks. He shook his head. "I hated that wind, but oddly, I miss it now.

"Master Witrin was my mentor, a solid, strong, kind man. He taught me almost everything I know: from the ancient texts of history, to the maps of the world, numbers, letters, and songs. As a child, I was sure he must know everything.

"He was the one who gave me my name. If I had a name before I came to them, they didn't know it. He named me Ahrn, after the Vanished God, Aehryn.

"Then there was Master Elia..."

Silence.

Senia took a moment to let his words sink in. A warm breeze blew across the rolling hills, tousling long golden grasses.

"What about you?" he said at last. The afternoon was wearing on, and they'd be stopping soon. The sun was low in the west, long shadows playing across the waving fields of grass. "What was your life like?"

There was a stab in her heart as she thought of her family. Though... perhaps it would help to talk about them.

"I came to live at the smithy when I was six."

"Odd," he said with the high-pitched voice of remembrance. That's the age I was when I came to the abbey." He gave a soft, "huh" and was quiet again.

It was odd, though purely coincidence, certainly. "Suddenly I had two older brothers, an older sister, and a younger brother and sister. You talk about the winds and the cold, but the one thing I remember is the warmth. Even in winter it was always warm. True we had a forge fire burning beneath us, but it was more than that, the closeness of the family, the chaos of children and chores, always something to do, someone to talk to." She had to stop there, her throat tight, tears welling.

She swallowed, took a moment, and once again, felt the tranquil soothing as Emberthorn touched her spirit.

There now child, all is well.

She went on. "I learned about many things in that house. As a girl, I learned with the girls, sewing, cooking, singing, laughing. Yet I was taller than any other girl in the village and strong enough that I could also help in the forge, learning crafting, cursing, weapons, horses, and the world of men."

The kernel of a memory came to her. "I remember, a couple years ago, my father and mother sitting with me in the kitchens. The other children had been put in their rooms to sleep, but I remained up. They told me of my real parents that night. Apparently, my adopted mother and my birth mother had been close friends, growing up in a village to the south. When a handsome journeyman smith had come through town, my adopted mother fell in love, and had moved along with him until they had set up a shop in Alindale, my village. My birth parents, both strong of will and body, had become mercenaries, working for the King, going where he commanded. They died, together, in a battle with the armies of Thania. Apparently, I have my mother's eyes and her hair, but my father's straight nose and brow."

She was quiet for a while then, basking in the memory.

Finally, she let out a long sigh, releasing the remembrance.

Ahrn turned to her, his eyes, catching the light of the setting sun, were gold, pure.

"You said yesterday, something about how we've both lost a lot recently. Now that I think about it that may be true, but... I think I'm glad that I had so much in my life up until now."

She nodded. It was true. She wasn't quite sure where her next words came from, but once said, the simply felt right. "At least we have each other now."

He smiled wide, his eyes sparkling. He took her free hand in his, as he'd done yesterday and gave it a squeeze.

"Each other," he said.

*a*hrn woke with the first rays of sun.

He'd slept well, despite hard earth as his bed. Senia was still and quiet, huddled under her cape, curled into a ball. Emberthorn's hilt, held in both hands was drawn up close to her face, the cat's head pommel nuzzled into her cheek. It didn't look comfortable, but then he wasn't the one forever bound to the massive sword.

The morning was warm for the season, a breeze ruffling the long grasses around them

He rose and tried some exercises to remove any aches and kinks from his body. The monks had several calisthenics they ran through daily to keep them in fighting shape. He removed his shirts after a while as he began to sweat. Once warmed and stretched, he moved through his fighting forms.

He had missed his morning practice for a few days running now, and after recalling how easily the big man had laid him low the previous day, he was certain he needed the refresher.

Honestly, he shouldn't have been caught so off guard. He blamed himself. He hadn't fought a commoner in ages and, in this case, had highly underestimated the speed of a man so large.

So, he practiced.

There were hundreds of forms and connecting movements which the warrior monks had picked up over the years. It was said that Embreth knew all of the secret styles of fighting developed over the ages and gave unto her monks the most effective and efficient to use. There was little show or flourish in the movements, they were meant to quickly disable or kill any who threatened the secrets of Embreth.

Senia woke as he was starting his second set of forms. Her eyes fluttering open, looking over at him.

"What are you doing?" she asked, sitting up and stretching.

"This is how the monks train for combat," he said, sliding from 'striking falcon' into 'weaving snake.'

"But you aren't fighting anyone."

He stopped. "No, but there are a series of moves we can practice even without an opponent so that when it comes time to fight, we don't need to think about what to do, our bodies will know what move is best to defeat the enemy." Oddly, that was almost the exact wording Master Elia used to describe the forms to new monks.

"Oh." Senia stood, rolling her shoulders, and stretching her arms out to the sides. Both movements had the effect

of pulling her shirt taut across her breasts. He felt a stirring deep within him, low and heated. It was odd, he had
lived with many other women, seen some completely
unclothed, and yet all had affected him little. Senia,
however, with the barest of movements, could arouse a
great rolling, knotted ache in the depths of his being.
Sometimes at very inopportune times... like now.

"Could you teach me?" she asked.

"It took me fifteen years, practicing every day for hours
on end to get to where I am. Master Elia says I'm one of her
best students. I can teach you, but understand there is a lot
to learn, it will take time."

"How long of a journey is it to this abbey?"

Ahrn shrugged. He knew the maps, but to say how
long it would take when he didn't know exactly where they
were now would be tough. "It is a two-month journey from
our abbey in the south to St. Antin Abbey. We were just
over a month on our way when we were attacked. I would
say it is three or four weeks away. We will pass through the
plains we're on now into forested hills, which will grow
higher for some time. The hills mark the border between
Aestria and Vohria to the north. Those hills are also the
foothills of a small mountain range known as Maalkin's
Rise." She smiled at the name. She would have known it
well as Maalkin was the God of stones, metals, and crafting. "After the foothills, there will be a great forest through
a long valley. Past the forest is Hallania, then it is up
another set of hills to the abbey."

"Three weeks to learn what took you most of your life."
She seemed skeptical.

"You could start." He shrugged.

"Perhaps, for now, I'll just watch."

"Fair enough. That's how I started."

She accepted that, brushing her long auburn hair back over a shoulder. The heat awakened within him again. All it took was the simplest things.

He took a moment to close his eyes and still his mind. This helped alleviate the arousal stirring within, and he began to move again.

He finished the second set and moved on through the third and fourth. He stopped there, not wanting to delay their journey.

As they ate a small meal, preparing to leave, she asked, "Is that all the moves?"

"No, that was three sets, there are twelve in total."

Her eyes widened. "It must take you a while to do them all."

He nodded.

She looked down at Emberthorn, across her lap. "Perhaps I'll just stick with him for now."

They made their way through the long grasses, following the north road.

For five more days they followed the road through fields, passing some small villages, but as the plains turned to rolling hills, it became apparent that the road was little used. What was a wide dirt road, became overgrown wagon tracks, and after they had passed one village on the edge of a small forest, it became little more than a path through the wilderness.

Ahrn continued to show Senia more of the forms every

morning. She watched, studiously, but never joined him. They talked more as they traveled, for it would have been a long, lonely journey otherwise, learning more of each other. He began to feel like he knew her, like he had known her for some time. There was something, some deep connection which, as he found out more about her, only grew stronger.

She still managed to cause that same ache, stirring his emotions with such small ordinary things, but over time the ache settled, became comforting, known, a constant companion just as she was.

CHAPTER 7

*A*s day faded to night, on their seventh day out, they stopped in a small valley between two rolling hills, making a small fire under the rustling leaves of a tall oak.

Ahrn sat back against the oak, a perfect spot to rest, a crook in the tree between two massive roots, cradling his back. He rested his head against the rough bark and watched the flames of sunset, then the first stars of night.

He was about to close his eyes when Senia's voice, low and husky, filled the silence around them.

"Why can't I let go?"

He looked over to her.

Head down, long hair pulled back over one shoulder glinting with light from the fire, she was intent on Emberthorn sitting, as ever, across her lap. That comforting warmth filled him at the sight of her, and he took in a long breath, letting the feeling bubble around inside him, savoring it.

"Let go?"

She looked up at him, brilliant eyes catching the fire-light, then back down again. "Of him."

"Who?"

She was stroking the blade of the sword, as she did whenever they sat.

"Emberthorn."

"Ah." Now he understood. In truth, though the monks knew much about the history of the Guardians, there was little information on the interactions of one with his or her artifact. He had noticed that the blade had rarely left her hands, was never put down, never released, no matter how awkward that made things for her. He had assumed it was part of the bonding, and it would seem that was true.

There was one thing he had heard though. "I recall reading of the great force of will contained within these artifacts. They require someone of equally great will to tame them."

She grimaced. "You have no idea."

"You let it go that first morning, when you..." He wasn't sure he wanted to remind her of losing her family, how fresh that wound may still be.

"It's odd. I didn't think about it then, as I don't think about holding him all the rest of the time. It's natural. Yet..." she paused, gritting her teeth, obvious frustrated. "Yet, if it was natural," she said slowly, "wouldn't I be able to release him whenever I wished?"

Ahrn was about to comment on this when she blew out a sigh and said, "Shut up, I'm not talking to you right now."

"What did it say?"

"'IT' is a 'HE', just so you know."

"Sorry, what did he say?"

"Something about being a work of perfection and why would anyone ever want to let him go. His words not mine."

"He seems to have a very well-defined personality."

She nodded. "You have no idea."

They both laughed a little. The mirth died quickly, though, her lips tight.

She got up, all swift grace, reversed her grip, and slammed the sword a good foot into the ground. Ahrn started at the sudden movement.

Then she stood there for a moment, her tan shirt and long brown skirt settling around her lithe form. Her hair had flared around her as she rose, and it floated, weightless for a long moment, before falling in wisps back to her shoulders and back. In the dancing light, she was the image of strength and beauty.

The warm bubbles billowed and popped. His breath taken.

One hand fell to her side. The other, after a long moment of staring intently at it, simply trembled, still holding the hilt.

"Why?"

Ahrn rose, approaching her tentatively.

She looked up, pleading, then back down at the blade. "Please."

He wasn't sure whether she was talking to him or Emberthorn.

"I just need to be... me, free for a moment."

He set his hand softly on hers, the one still on Emberthorn, feeling the soft skin, fine fingers.

Her eyes rose to his then.

"I didn't ask for this."

"No, you didn't." He tore his gaze from the amazing, azure depths within hers and looked down at the sword. "Emberthorn, I don't know if you can hear or understand me, but please let her go."

"I've tried asking, but he says he can't help it. He says it's up to me."

Ahrn looked back up into those wide pleading pools. Then he stepped in between her and the sword. This brought him so close to her, their faces mere whispers apart. His one hand still behind him on hers on Emberthorn, he brought his other up to her face, brushing stray hairs back.

The warm bubbles burst, igniting a fire within him, his body responding to their nearness.

"Concentrate on me, then." He was lost in her eyes. Her scent, fresh lavender, wrapped around him. "Focus on my eyes." His heart was racing. A billow of wind brushed her skirt against the fabric of his pants, the cloths kissing lightly. His free hand settled on her shoulder and, to his amazement, she relaxed.

He worked carefully now, trying to fill her attention, while slowly, lightly removing her fingers, one by one from the hilt of the sword behind him.

He slid his hand down her arm to her hand, grasping it. "Feel my strength, use it. Forget about everything that has happened."

She closed her eyes, concentrating.

The loss of those azure depths—that break from her intensity—sent him reeling.

"How can I forget any of this?" she whispered, voice hoarse, heavy.

"By remembering who you are. Senia, a strong, kind woman of pure heart and innocent beauty."

Her eyes snapped open, capturing him yet again. "You think I'm beautiful?"

He froze, caught by the question. Had he really just said that? What was he doing?

"Oh!" she breathed.

"What?"

"My hand." He looked and indeed, her hand was free of the hilt, held in his at their side. He hadn't noticed, so caught up had he been in the moment.

She smiled at him. Then quickly leaned in, pressing soft lips to his for a heartbeat. Releasing, but still close, she whispered, "thank you."

In the next instant, she broke away from him, dancing a few steps, twirling, arms outstretch beneath the starlight.

Ahrn tried not to think too hard about the last few moments or the way his body had responded to her kiss.

"Anything for you," he whispered, barely a breath of sound, sure she never heard it in her reveling. Then he returned to his seat in the crook of the oak tree.

He tried to close his eyes, but when he did, all he saw was her, close and wondrous. So, he stared into the fire as if the flames might burn away her image.

Eventually, she came to sit by him, legs crossed. Both him and the fire were between her and the sword.

"Emberthorn is a gift, an amazing thing," she said. "But sometimes I need to remember who I am." She was quiet for a moment, then said again, "Thank you."

They sat together under the gathering night in silence as the fire died.

It grew chill. She got up to retrieve her cape, which she'd left near Emberthorn. She returned, wrapped in its warmth, and again sat next to him, watching the flickering embers.

"Tell me about this place we're going to."

He looked over at her shadowed form. "St. Antin Abbey is a great fortress. I made a pilgrimage there once when I was twelve. I remember little other than walls so high they seemed like they brushed the sky, and so many people. Hundreds of monks live there, so many more than my small abbey."

"Will I be safe there?"

"As safe as anywhere, and safer than most. The monks there are well-trained and as I said, the walls are high and strong."

"And... will you stay there with me?"

"I..." His voice caught. Of course he would... wouldn't he? That had been his destination before all of this began. But... could he stay so close to her? Could he remain this close and keep his vows? "I don't know."

She turned to him then, eyes bright in the darkness. "I hope you will." She turned away again quickly.

He was at a complete loss. Words came and went,

unspoken. He needed to tell her of his vows, his duty. Yet other words warred with these, professions of feelings, of how much he wanted to stay with her, close to her. There was no victor but silence.

"Thank you," she said again, voice quiet. "For everything. For helping me." She turned to him in the dimness. "You didn't know me, and..." Soft, breathy laughter. "Look at us now. It seems silly, but, right now, you're all I have."

"You have Emberthorn."

She shot him a sour look. "That's not funny."

It hadn't been meant as funny.

"Emberthorn is always... ever-so-close. I can feel him even now when separated from him. Even now, he calls to me. But..." She reached out laying a hand on Ahrn's outstretched leg. He felt her warmth through the fabric of his cloak and pants. "...There is little warmth in his embrace."

After a moment, she looked at her hand on his leg and it flinched away, hovering for a moment before sliding back under her cape. A part of him went with her.

"I'm sorry. I..."

"No, no need to be sorry." He didn't know where these words were coming from, but he no longer wished to stop them. He held out his hand from under his own cloak. "I understand."

She smiled, her own hand emerging to take his. Then she shuffled herself over next to him, close, pushing him to one side of the crook in the oak tree. Oddly, it fit two much better than one. She lay her head on his shoulder, their joined hands between them, her body snuggled close, and that is where she drifted off to sleep.

For a moment, Ahrn struggled with his vows. Yet, nothing had happened. They were growing close, yes, but he was close with lots of women. Satisfied for the moment, he closed his eyes and found, now, the image of her face comforted him.

CHAPTER 8

*S*enia! *Someone is coming, wake now!*
　　Emberthorn's call was clear and crisp in her mind, so much more than that first night, when it had seemed as if he'd been calling from a great distance.

She opened her eyes, finding her arms around Ahrn, remembering the comfort he'd offered, the warmth of his body.

Loss and sorrow surged through her, still keen-edged, but there was something fresh, something that had been blossoming over these last few days, something which was starting to soothe and dull the ache of losing her family.

Suddenly Emberthorn's words struck home. Someone was coming. She rose quickly and, running to Emberthorn, called back to Ahrn, "Wake up!"

Every movement she made when not in contact with the sword seemed slow, like moving through a dense wind or with enfeebled muscles. Also, her senses were dim, the night too dark, the sounds and scents muted.

Yet as soon as her fingers touched the hilt, power and strength rushed into her, and she plucked the blade easily from the ground. Her night-sight returned, and everything lightened around her. A symphony of scents and sounds surrounded her: crickets keening, the tang of smoldering ash, Ahrn's heady musk of earth and sweat.

She raised the sword, waiting, watching, listening.

Ahrn came awake. "What? Senia?" He peered around in the darkness before his eyes settled on her. "Is that you?"

"Yes, someone is coming." As she said it, she heard them. Barely more than a rustling of the grass, but it was too regular to be the wind. Whoever it was, they wished not to be heard, nor seen. Her heart raced. This meant only one thing.

"Assassins," she breathed.

With her next breath, they flooded out of the night, so many of them. Ahrn was up quickly. They reached him first, her a moment after.

Emberthorn cried out, enflamed by the attack, and she let him take control of her. She may not wish to kill, but ever so much more than that, she wanted to live.

Three were down around her with a quick step and a slash of the long blade. Others were moving around her.

She heard a faint sound, discordant, clicking.

She knew the sound, but it was a faint memory, Emberthorn knew it better. The crank of a crossbow.

"Ahrn, move!" she cried, and with a strength born from some as of yet unknown reserve, she launched herself high into the night. She'd been able to pinpoint the exact location of the crossbowman by the sound, and she landed many yards from where she had been, next to the man. He released his bolt too quickly, and she heard the thud of it impacting the oak tree. With a quick stroke of her blade, the archer was no longer a concern.

In the stillness between the beats of her heart, she listened intently. It was amazing. She sensed no other archers, just the one, and could locate every one of the attackers, all sixteen remaining.

She ran, as a hunting cat rushes its prey, and pounced on a small group waiting to get close to Ahrn.

Two died with one slice, two more with the next. Again, she took a half-heartbeat to watch Ahrn fight, weaponless, using this opponent's weapons and movement against them. He did not possess the preternatural senses and abilities she gained through Emberthorn, instead having spent hours upon hours for days and years practicing to achieve such fluidity and flow. She marveled at this skill.

The next moment she returned her attention to the attackers. It was a deadly dance, with Emberthorn as her partner, moving as one, beauteous in its devastation.

Something became apparent very quickly. These men had no idea how to fight a Scion. But from what Ahrn had told her, that made sense. Since no Guardians had fought on this earth for hundreds of years. No one knew how to deal with what she was. For an instant, she could understand how men must have feared the Guardians and why they rose up against them.

Another enemy fell before her as wheat before a

thresher. She spun to seek more, but none were there. Ahrn was finishing with the last, the attacker's short blade somehow reversed and thrust through his own stomach. He fell with a surprised look in his eyes.

I had forgotten the glory of righteous battle. Emberthorn sighed within her.

Still, she wasn't used to such carnage. But it was only now, as the sword's battle-fever ebbed, that it truly sunk in. Looking around at the scattered blood and gore, disgust and pity welled up within her.

She dropped to her knees, bile burning her throat. She stopped herself from being sick, but only barely. It was a moment later, when she realized that the warm ground beneath her knees was actually blood soaking into her skirt, that she was sick.

Afterwards, she rose unsteadily and staggered away into darkness. She needed to get away, someplace distant, clean, and pure, and where life and goodness abounded. She made it to just the other side of one of the hills around them before collapsing in tears.

That was where Ahrn found her.

He knelt next to her, laying a warm, comforting hand on her back. "Senia? Are you well?"

She shook her head.

"What can I get you?"

"Water, then away from here."

"I'll be right back." He rose and walked away, and in that moment, she realized what it was she had really wanted. Him simply being close to her. Now, in the cold of night, her emotions in turmoil, she wanted his

warmth, his hand on her back as it had been, perhaps…
more.

I don't want to be around for that part, Emberthorn said
warily.

What part?

I know what you're thinking.

What was I thinking?

Not something I can repeat in polite company.

*I hardly think you're polite company. You just killed thirteen
men.* And she could remember each of them. Masked as
they were, she knew not their faces, only their eyes, but
each set was burned into her memory. Evil or no, they
were still men, men she had killed.

*Killing is one thing, but what you're thinking is something
else entirely. As I said, you can release me if that's what you
have in mind.*

I still don't know what you're talking about.

Emberthorn gave an odd laugh. *You are so very young
and pure, aren't you? You don't even know what your own
deepest desires are.*

What are they?

Not my place to say, sorry.

Now you're just being annoying.

She wasn't quite sure how she knew, but Emberthorn
was smiling cryptically.

"Fine, be that way."

"What way? Or are you talking Emberthorn again?"
Ahrn had returned. She groaned. "Here's some water," he
said lowering a waterskin, kneeling next to her again.

She released Emberthorn and took the offered water.

Releasing Emberthorn seemed rather easy this time; perhaps it was her infuriation with him.

The first sip she used to rinse out her mouth, spitting it out, and wiping her mouth. Then she took several long swigs, to refresh herself.

"Thank you."

"Not really used to battle, are you?"

"I was a normal girl before we met, remember? Where would I have gotten used to battle?"

"Understood. I'm sorry that this is being forced on you."

She looked up at him then, her eyes calm and kind. "What was your first time like?"

"I was ten."

"By all the Gods, that young?"

He nodded. "I didn't kill anyone in the first fight, but I broke a man's leg. I can still remember the sound. I too was rather sick that night."

She grimaced. "Thank you, that makes me feel a little better."

Again, his hand touched her back, this time stroking widely across her shoulders. "I'm sorry," he said again. He looked away. "This is all my fault."

She let out a clipped, hard laugh. "You did bring Emberthorn into my village." He tensed, his hand freezing on her back. "But you couldn't have known what that would begin. This is not your fault Ahrn. This is Reisha of the Fates playing a game with all of us."

He relaxed a little and resumed caressing her shoulders.

She pushed herself up from her hands and knees, sitting on her feet. She reached a hand to his face. There was a few days of beard on his chin, rough on her fingers. Again, that deep feeling, which had mingled with and soothed her grief and loss, welled up within her. She felt a lump grow in her throat, tears in her eyes. Suddenly his nearness, his warmth was all that mattered to her.

"Ahrn, will you... will you hold me?" she asked around the lump in her throat.

He hesitated.

Finally, nodding, he gathered her up in strong arms, leaning her into him, her head on his shoulder. Even without Emberthorn's advanced senses, this close, she could smell his deep scent of sweat and earth. He laid his cheek on her forehead.

"This will all be over soon. We'll get to St. Antin Abbey, and you'll be all right. You'll be safe."

After a moment, he added a soft, "hush now," as he slowly stroked her back. She hadn't even realized she'd been weeping again, so safe and warm she felt in his embrace.

She moved her head then, feeling the hot tears on her cheek shift direction. She tilted upward as he turned to her. So close their noses touched.

Her heart ached, longing, singing for him to be even closer still. She brushed her lips over his and felt them respond, pushing down onto hers, opening with hers, the kiss deepening an unfathomable connection.

The world faded and there was only warmth, perfection. Her heart gave itself over to the moment as everything within her joined with him. This was right, pure, filling the void within her.

She slid her arms out from her cape and under his cloak, feeling the hard muscles of his back move beneath his shirt as he shifted his arms. His soft touch caressed her hair, following its flow to her shoulder and down her back.

His eyes, golden suns, burned into her with their intensity. Her soul pulled, responded to his passion. Their faces pressed ever closer, lips wet. Her body moved of its own whim, folding into him, feeling the heat of his body as the bare fabric of their clothes brushed between them. The chill of the night was gone, there was only heat filling her from the core outward, pooling deep within and radiating to every pore.

She laid back, pulling him down onto her, their cape and cloak as entwined as their bodies. His hands molded to her, taking every sweep and curve of her body in their touch. His lips left hers and moved to her cheek, chin, neck, and lower still, his deft fingers pulling the strings on her shirt, to give him room to explore.

A moan welled up from the depths of her soul. An upheaval of grief, loss, sorrow, passion, and joy. With it everything released. She squeezed her eyes shut, feeling tears run rivers down to her ears.

His lips froze, still pressed to the swell of a breast.

"No."

He shuddered and drew back sharply. As he left, so went her breath, sucked from her. She arched toward him, lifting, needing his embrace. Her body strung like a fiddle, waiting to sing at his touch.

"No." He pushed himself away, rising quickly. "I can't."

Air returned with a ragged, painful series of clipped gasps. Slowly, unwillingly, she lay back down, the heat and longing, the intense need burning within her, little cooled by a passing night's breeze.

"I'm sorry," he said, sitting next to her, but looking away. His voice was hoarse, torn. "I... I have vows to my God. I... I'm so sorry." Choked, he rose quickly, striding several steps away.

Eventually, Senia steadied her breath, the intensity of the moment fading. The desire lingered, remaining, waiting, a hidden bonfire undisturbed by the raging storm of emotions around it.

She rolled to her side, collecting her cape around her. Tears gathered again, rolling down her cheeks, weeping quietly. She wouldn't let him know her pain. He had his vows and she, for the moment, was left with nothing.

She pulled her knees up, hugging them tight, and wept silently until exhaustion took her. She sunk into dreamless oblivion which brought little release or relief.

CHAPTER 9

*A*hrn couldn't sleep, though it seemed that Senia was soon resting.

He wasn't sure what he had expected. Protest, anger, tears? But he had expected something. Instead, she had quietly rolled over and gone to sleep.

His heart was torn, broken and seeping. He loved this woman who he hardly knew. He didn't know how it was possible, but she had, within the span of a week, nearly caused him to throw away everything he held dear in his life.

The scary thing was, he still wanted to throw it all away. He wanted to go back to her, to shatter his life, his vows, and be with her.

He had thought for that brief moment she had felt the same way, that she would call him back. He would have come, given up everything. Yet she never did. So, with the passing of the chill breeze of the night, eventually his passion cooled.

He spent the night dealing with the bodies.

He remembered bits of the fight as he did, and from the remains of the bodies managed to figure out the rest. He had to admit that the battle-prowess of a Scion, even one who was untrained, was breathtaking.

It took him hours to dig a long low trench using a small spade he'd found on one of the bodies, but he didn't mind the work. It was invigorating and took his mind off of Senia and his vows to Embreth.

As dawn began to seep into the east, he was mostly done filling in the grave. He finished as the sun rose, brilliant and clean, the sky fresh and clear.

He gathered up his pack and added a few small items, including the spade collected from The Blacklord's men. He put together Senia's small bundle as well and strode over the hill to where she slept, curled into a ball.

God, her clothes were a mess. He hadn't noticed, even with his extreme proximity last night. Mud and blood, so much blood, mostly long streams but some large pools, covered her in a patchwork.

He did not wake her but sat by her instead. He gazed upon her as the first rays of sun brushed her hair and cheek. The light brought out the red and shimmers of blond in her hair, her cheek, blushed and perfect, her lips...

He turned away.

He couldn't even look at her now without feeling the passion rekindle. So instead, he watched the light spread over the countryside. The morning was beautiful, almost as beautiful as the woman behind him he could no longer even think of without flames licking his already burned heart.

Somehow, he couldn't enjoy the splendor around him that day. He looked up at the sky and asked his God why she couldn't have given him a dark and gray day to match his mood, to remind him of Her and his vows... his infernal vows.

He grew more restless as the morning wore on and had worked himself into a foul mood by the time Senia woke.

Silent, she rose and retrieved Emberthorn and her own belongings.

They left.

As they walked through the morning, Senia was cool, distant. He couldn't blame her, but it did little to help his dark thoughts.

Late morning found them entering a stretch of woods, and shortly after noon they came to a river cutting through the forest. The road crossed the burbling waters at a shallow point, no more than a foot or two deep.

They ate a meager lunch at the ford, then Senia muttered something about needing to bathe and clean her clothes. She followed the river down and around a bend out of sight.

Since they had seen no other traffic on this road, which was now little more than a path winding northward, Ahrn saw no need to wander off to do the same thing. He stripped down, washing his shirt, pants, and cloak, setting them on a branch, which caught the sun, to dry. He splashed water over himself, trying as best he could with raw hands to scrub the dirt and sweat away. Then he dried himself with a small rag in his pack and tended to a few small wounds he'd taken last night, binding them tightly. He used the reflection in the water to shave as best he could then dressed in a second set of rough brown shirt and pants, his only other set of clothes.

He was just beginning to wonder what was taking Senia so long, when a high crisp scream echoed through the woods from her direction.

He sprinted, leaping roots, branches tearing at him, splashing through the banks of the river where no path in the forest was clear, to the bend in the river... and stopped, stiff.

There she was, naked, hip-deep in the river. The water, like a low-slung dress, flirted with the curve of her buttocks and played around the tops her legs. He drew his eyes upwards, over slender waist, high round breasts, long slender arms, and elegant neck, meeting her eyes as she noticed him.

She gave another hushed yelp and dropped herself into the water. She came up a moment later, as far as her chin.

"Sorry," Senia said, blushing furiously, eyes sheepish.

Ahrn was still stunned, unable to speak, her body burned in his memory, an image of perfection.

"It's been a while since I bathed in a river." Her words came out in a rush. "I forgot about the fish. One of them brushed by me... it startled me. I didn't mean to alarm you."

"Oh," was all Ahrn could manage in reply. He didn't move.

They stared at each other, eyes locked. A strong breeze washed through the trees above them. Neither one of them moved.

"I'm good now."

"Good."

Ahrn couldn't think of anything else to say. His tongue moistened his lips, knowing he should say... something. The moment stretched.

"You can go now."

"Yes," he said, realizing only then he should have left some time ago. He turned away, breaking the spell of the scene, and walked slowly back to the road. By all the Gods, what an idiot he must seem to her. Breaking away last night then completely unable to do so today.

His heart raced, partly from the scare and the dash through the forest, but mostly from the remembrance of her.

He reached the road and sat, waiting. Trying desperately to get his thoughts, his entire life, back in order. Everything was falling apart around him, within him, and he wasn't sure he wanted it to stop.

Senia stepped onto the road a little while later, hair wet, clinging to her, soaking through the thin fabric of her white linen shirt. It was a new shirt. She'd had a spare set of clothes, but only the one cape. It was slung over an arm, still drying, the blood spots now just faint brown scars on the cloth.

He didn't know what he could say that would make

him seem any less like a confused, obsessed, distracted dolt, so he said nothing. They started off in silence and so it was for the remainder of the day.

CHAPTER 10

*T*he next week of traveling seemed to stretch, drawn into an unending rise of higher and higher hills, and little companionship. Senia had begun to feel close to Ahrn, linked somehow, but since that night... after the fight... and the day at the river, that had all changed. He was distant now, saying little, only what was needed to be polite, but never anything deeper. He was cut off to her and she could feel it, as if an arm or leg had been removed. No, not a limb, something internal. She could survive without an arm, but she felt like she was quietly dying, some inner piece of her torn out, leaving a bloody trail behind her to those places where everything had changed.

Couldn't he feel what they had shared in that kiss? Didn't he see how they were joined now?

Apparently not.

They came to a city.

"Riston," Ahrn said, emotionless. How he knew, he didn't share, as it was with everything now.

"Anything I need to know before we go down there?" She hoped perhaps to elicit some response from him. They stood on a high rise, overlooking the city, which sat sprawled down the side of the hill opposite them in the valley to the edge of a wide river which cut the valley floor. It was just after noon.

"Women with swords will be rare, you'll be out of place with that." He vaguely waved his hand in the direction of Emberthorn.

I don't like it when he calls me 'that'. Emberthorn, perhaps feeling her pain, was pouty.

I know. He doesn't mean it, I'm sure. He's just upset right now.

Because you kissed? I'm still a little fuzzy on that one.

Senia sighed. *It's his vows.*

You've mentioned that.

They are important to him. They are his life, and I'm threatening them. So, he's angry at me, or himself, or something... I don't know. I don't really know what's going on at all and he doesn't seem interested in telling me. Have I mentioned I don't really want to talk about it?

Then why is it all you think about?

Because I can think about whatever I want and not have to talk about it, that's how things are supposed to work when you don't have a sword with a mind of its own in your head.

Right, sorry.

Ahrn started down the ridge toward the city. "We need

supplies, we'll have to go through, so figure out what you are doing with that beast of a weapon."

She frowned at him, sticking her tongue out for a moment. It was childish, but that didn't stop it from feeling good.

Senia walked after him but made no effort to catch up.

Any thoughts on how I can hide you?

Why would you want to?

You heard what he said.

I did, but that doesn't mean he's making any sense.

She gave Emberthorn a mental frown of displeasure.

Fine, there is something.

I'm listening.

There is a command. If you say 'Float' you will not need to hold me, I'll just hover along next to you.

And that won't draw any attention at all. She rolled her eyes.

There is another command, but I don't like it much.

Tell me.

I don't want to.

Tell me now, Emberthorn. I am your Guardian, and I need to know. She wasn't being kind, but then again, she was already aggravated, and he wasn't helping.

Emberthorn sighed heavily. *Sometimes you're no fun at all.*

Emberthorn!

You can tell me to 'Vanish' and I'll disappear.

Great, Van...

Wait!

What?

Not yet, please.

Why?

Because. She felt Emberthorn shudder, his fear leaving the taste of ash in her mouth. *It's... a dark, lonely place I go to. I don't like it there.*

Senia let out a long sigh. *Fine, I'll wait.*

Thank you.

How do I get you back?

Say my name, out loud.

She nodded. *Can I still talk to you when you're 'vanished'?*

No. You are essentially breaking our connection in a way. It is something Guardians only rarely did. It hurts both of us.

This was turning out to be a grand day indeed.

Farther down the hill, when within sight of the ferry that would take them across the river to the city, she told Emberthorn to vanish... and fell to her knees when she did.

Ahrn, still walking ahead, didn't notice.

For a moment, the pain was unbearable, shuddering through her body in waves. It quickly subsided to a general ache, a deep muscle soreness throbbing through her. As she rose, heavily, there was a stab of pain in her side, muscles cramping. She bent, sucking air through clenched teeth until it stopped, but she found, as she staggered down the rest of the hill, that such sharp points of pain would come and go, punctuating the ache that was her body.

When she joined Ahrn at the edge of the river, he glanced over at her, then, turned to her, confused.

"Where...?"

"Gone, don't ask." Her foul mood had increased with the pain, his bewildered look gave her a moment's joy.

He shrugged, peering back up the hill, then turned back to her with a nod. "Good."

No, not good. Couldn't he see she was in agony!

The ferry came.

The river was wide and sluggish here, the simple barge, large and flat, had several strong men poling them across. Senia, having lost the exceptional balance she possessed with Emberthorn and already feeling slightly ill, sat on the deck, the slight sway and pitch threatening to make a really bad day worse. Ahrn seemed fine, standing steady. She glared at him in that moment, loathing his easy grace and strength.

She forced herself to walk off the barge, crawling would just have been too much to bear.

The unmoving earth was much better, but her head was swimming now, either a further consequence of sending Emberthorn away, or a lingering side-effect of the ferry-ride, she wasn't sure.

The first thing on this side of the river was a wide, well-worn road, east to west. On the other side of that a great and bustling market. Beyond the stalls and wagons buildings began, the city looming over them, seeming taller for the hill that it climbed.

Senia nearly lost her lunch.

One dry convulsion and she steadied herself.

Ahrn was there, firm hand on her back. "Are you unwell?"

Eyes clamped shut to control her traitorous body, she couldn't see him, but he actually sounded concerned.

"No!" she said through clenched teeth.

"I know of some herbs for sea-sickness."

No, that wasn't it, and she knew it now. It was something else, something greater. The connection between her and Emberthorn had grown strong and to be without him was harsh and painful.

And she'd be damned if she let Ahrn see it.

She straightened slowly, jaw trembling from the force of ramming her teeth together. "I'll... be... fine," she gasped. A long breath, then. "Let's get our supplies and go."

He nodded. He did look concerned, honey-eyes soft and drawn.

"If you want, you can rest while I get what we need. I shouldn't be long."

She shook her head.

He perked up suddenly. "I could find a room for the night, you could have a bed?"

She shook her head violently; she didn't want to stay in the city any longer than she had to. As long as she was here, she was without Emberthorn.

And that was torture.

"Oh..." This seemed to throw him. "We'll just get the supplies, and we'll go then?"

She tried a smile. "Thank you." It didn't come out kindly, but then she wasn't in any sort of a 'kindly' way at the moment.

She followed him into the market.

People clustered around her, tight, airless, loud.

She stopped to steady herself on the side of a fruit stand, and when she looked up, Ahrn was gone.

There was movement all around, her vision swam, people's faces bobbing and babbling in a never-ending sea, then...

A flash of black.

It couldn't be. Not here, and yet, she knew the assassins would stop at nothing to take her.

"Emb..." Choked, breathless. A strong arm wrapped around her neck, squeezing the air out of her. Too late, far, far too late.

Ahrn appeared, seeing her, his eyes grew wide.

Something dug sharply into her side. A voice, behind her, low and quiet, said, "Don't move, monk, or she dies."

Ahrn, a growing helplessness drawing his features, raised his hands out to the side. Several black-clad men came into view, grabbing him.

The pressure on her neck increased, and her world faded.

Her last image was Ahrn, his voice unheard, his lips forming the words, "I'm sorry, Senia."

CHAPTER 11

*S*enia lay, pallid, sprawled where the men in black had tossed her, on the cold stone floor of the keep.

Ahrn watched everything, waiting, keeping his rage bottled for the moment. He would kill these men, of that he was sure, but for now, something larger was happening, and he needed to pay attention.

The group of ten men who'd captured them in the market were augmented by a further score of black-clad men around the large hall. They were waiting for something or someone. A large wooden chair on a raised dais was the focal point of the room, made for the Lord of this city perhaps. Ahrn waited, a rope tight and raw on his wrists bound behind him.

The man who emerged from the curtain behind the throne was of average height, dressed in fine, thick robes, a rich dark blue with silver trim. His dark eyes, sharp and keen traced over Ahrn, then Senia, his brow raising slightly. He raised a hand to stroke the small patch of beard at his chin, neatly trimmed.

He strode to Ahrn, his gait confident, easy. They were of a height, Ahrn having the slight advantage, he met the man's gaze with stern, cold eyes.

"Where is the sword?" the man asked, his tone even, casual.

A cold, hard ball formed in the pit of Ahrn's stomach. "What sword?"

The man raised a hand before Ahrn's face and snapped his fingers. Searing pain spiked into Ahrn's eyes, he shut them against the blinding light, turning away.

"Do not make the mistake of believing that you are of any worth to me, monk," the man said, his voice still level, unfazed.

Ahrn should have known The Blacklord would send one of his puppet mages after Senia. Ahrn had little experience fighting against magic. This was not going to be fun.

Ahrn could hear the wizard's footfalls on the stone of the floor pacing around him. "I will kill you unless you are of use to me. So... what is it to be?"

Ahrn tried to open his eyes, seeing at first only massive dark splotches with a haze of the rest of the room around the edges. Slowly the spots faded, but he knew he wouldn't have full sight for some time yet.

"I told her to hide it. I didn't think a girl with a Greatsword would look right in a city."

"A sensible precaution. Where did she leave it?"

"I... I don't know."

With his blurry sight, Ahrn saw the wizard raise a

hand. He spun away from whatever magic might be coming. The bright bolt of white-hot light which streamed from the mage's palm only grazed his side and the side of his arm forced behind him. Still, he felt his skin burn, heard the sear. Pain shot through him.

He collapsed, trying as best he could, with hands tied, to protect his side.

"Do you expect me to believe that you wouldn't know such a thing? You a monk of Embreth, keeper of secrets?"

He grimaced, teeth clenched. "You can believe whatever you wish. You are obviously going to kill me, so why should I tell you anything."

"I can make this quick and easy or roast you gradually over the next week. Which would you prefer?"

"Either way I'm dead."

"True. It depends on how much pain you are willing to endure for this girl."

"I will never tell you where the sword is." It helped that he had no clue what Senia had actually done with the thing.

"We shall see." Without looking, Ahrn could tell from the rustling of the man's robes that he was kneeling next to where Ahrn lay.

Even turned away, eyes shut so tight tears squeezed from the rims, he could see the blossom of light next to his head. It was hot, and with torturous patience, the wizard pressed it closer. Hair singed away, his ear burned, shriveling, the entire side of his head, doused in fire.

He screamed. He couldn't help but release the pain in some way.

The burning stopped, the light fading, leaving only the acrid smell of his own charred flesh.

"Well, what say you, monk?"

"On the hill, across the river. There is a bush of thistles near the top, it's buried there."

The wizard pressed his hand into the burned flesh on Ahrn's face, causing another scream. He pushed down, though he need not use much force as Ahrn instinctively moved away until the other side of his face was pressed to the cold stone.

"I hope you aren't lying to me, monk." The hand released, and the rustling of fabric indicated the wizard was standing, moving away. "Go," the man called out. "Find the sword and bring it to me."

The lie would only buy time. Ahrn had to figure out what to do with that time.

He had to think, to move past the pain and do something.

Opening his eyes, well actually only one eye, for the other was partially burned, seared shut, he risked a glance out across the floor.

Senia lay directly in his field of view, not too far away and... awake.

She too, obviously sensing some risk, had only one eye open, the one closest to the floor, and she was looking at him. Though her face didn't alter, through the intense gaze, the wideness of the eye, the slight shudder of her brow, the tears emerging from that azure pool, he knew she could see the full extent of his injuries.

For a moment, which spanned no more than two beats

of his heart, an eternity of understanding passed between them. They shared the secrecy, the pain, the uncertainty of this moment.

Ahrn tried to shake his head ever so slightly, and she nodded, only the barest hint of movement. Then she closed her eye, remaining still.

Good, he had an ally. She might not have her sword, but perhaps, somehow, together they could get free from this place.

Through the agony, the blistering pain, Ahrn moved, pushing himself up until he had his knees beneath him, his forehead still pressing the stone floor.

'Wizard!" he croaked out. "What is your name?"

From some distance away the man replied, still ever so calm. "You wish to know the name of the man who will kill you, monk?"

"Perhaps I do."

"Prandol, Wizard of light and seeing, Archmage of The Blacklord."

"An Archmage, really? He sent one of his highest to get this little girl?"

"The highest. And I think we both know that this 'little girl' as you call her, is worth it. A prize unlike any other. A Scion with bonded Aehryn-Gift. We both also know she has, with rather surprising ease, dealt with the two forces that were sent against her so far. So yes, I was called in to oversee the capture of the Scion."

Good, get him talking, let him think he was in control. Ahrn rocked back onto bent knees, his side lancing pain as he tried to sit straight. He gritted through it.

"How did you find us?"

A laugh, light and easy. "Did I completely ruin your hearing monk? I'm a wizard of light and *seeing*. I have been following you for over a week now. It was pure providence that you happened to be heading straight for me."

That wasn't right. Heading straight for him? He had been here all along? "What would an Archmage of The Blacklord be doing in some city in Vohria?" Ahrn asked.

Looking over, from his kneeling position, Ahrn, with his one good eye, watched Prandol turn leisurely. The wizard raised a single brow with a sly smile. "I've been here for weeks now, overseeing the final stages of domination. The Blacklord came to an... agreement with the King of Vohria some time ago. They are... allies now, all of Vohria added to The Blacklord's realm. I have been here making sure the local lord was cooperating. This will be one of our staging grounds for an attack on your abbey of St. Antin. It will fall, and then there will be no united force against us." Prandol stalked over to Ahrn, bending low to sneer in his face. "I love being the bearer of bad news."

Ahrn swallowed a lump in his throat. Could the forces of The Blacklord be this far advanced, on the doorstep of St. Antin, with none of the monks knowing?

"And I love that you are so willing to tell me all this."

"Oh, and why is that?"

"Because, I'll have so much to report when I reach the abbey."

Prandol's sneer widened, curling into his cheeks. "You monks, always so confident. It's going to be such fun breaking you."

"The feeling is mutual."

"Pardon...?"

Ahrn rocked back on his feet and launched himself at the unsuspecting wizard. Head first, colliding into the man's jaw. He heard the wet slap of the jaw slamming shut, the few unsteady footfalls as the wizard staggered back, then collapsed.

Ahrn dropped back to the floor, rolled to his back, and though the rope at his wrists tore his flesh, he separated his hands far enough that he could squeeze them around his hips and feet. With hands in front of him, he kicked himself upright in one fluid movement and, hands still bound, bashed the side of the face of the guard who had come running to the aid of the wizard.

The room erupted into motion, all of it towards him. He smiled in the instant he had to himself before the next man rushed in. As he had hoped, Senia lay completely ignored, forgotten on the floor.

A sword flashed.

Ahrn spun, weaving to the side, catching the man's hands as the sword descended into the space where he had been. A knee to the attacker's gut, and the man released his blade long enough for Ahrn to take it. As the man folded from the knee strike, Ahrn brought the sword down hard, stabbing into the man's back.

The man froze, already dead but not yet knowing it. Ahrn released the sword, which remained as it was, stuck in the other man's back, then moved his tied hands to the blade. The keen edge slid through his bonds, and he was free.

Another man came. A snap-kick to the face sent him back into the man behind him, giving Ahrn time to deal with two men attacking from the other side. He side-kicked one man's blade into the other's, fouling them up. An elbow to the throat stopped another. Ahrn grabbed that man's hand, forcing his blade into the attacker next to him, whose wide eyes as he died suggested he'd never suspecting his death blow would come from an ally. Ahrn snapped the first man's neck and moved on.

After that, everything else was forgotten in the intense concentration of the fight. His pain, his feelings for Senia, his desire to see old friends alive still, all were subdued to the flow of the movements, the forms of the fight. The flood of the enemy crashed upon him, and he could do nothing but strive to survive.

CHAPTER 12

Senia heard the fight and opened her eyes.

With a quick turn of her head, she took in the room. No one was near her. They were all clustered around Ahrn, who fought desperately, his burned body hampering him little. The amount of will, of strength, it must have taken to fight with such injuries astounded Senia. Inspired, Senia rose to her feet.

The Guards must not have thought her a threat, or they had felt she would be unconscious for longer as they hadn't bound her. It would have mattered little anyway as soon as she had called back...

"Emberthorn." Feeling with every syllable of the word her strength return to her.

I'm back! The pure elation in Emberthorn's voice rocked her with joy, and as her emotions filtered to him as well, the pain, the anticipation of a fight, his enjoyment only grew.

Let's go help Ahrn shall we? She could sense the giant grin as he said the words.

"Yes, let's."

There was something different about this fight. An intensity which was apparent almost immediately. She hadn't wanted either of the previous two encounters, hadn't wanted to fight but had been forced to by Emberthorn or by necessity. But, having heard and seen the unbridled cruelty of this wizard, the pleasure he took while inflicting pain, this was a fight she walked into willingly. Something sparked within her which ignited and roared to life within Emberthorn as well. Flames erupted all over the six feet of steel that was Emberthorn's blade.

Oh, Senia! You don't know how good this feels!

Actually, yes, she did.

At the fight now, she cut a swath of men away from Ahrn. They fell, dead, their clothes smoldering. A primal need grew within her, to protect, to defend, to defeat those who brought pain and suffering to others.

Ahrn was forgotten by The Blacklord's men, no longer a significant threat compared to the she-demon wielding a flaming blade.

Senia danced. Leaping and spinning around the room. They quickly learned she could take several in one swing if they were close together, so they moved apart, darting in on at a time to attack her, or throwing weapons.

Several ran to get crossbows from a weapons rack in the back corner of the room.

After felling the last of the foul villains nearby, she

leapt to Ahrn's side. She easily knocked aside a knife thrown her way and said,

"How are you? I think it best if we left soon. More will come."

"I can walk." The pain in his voice was palpable, heavy.

"Then let's do that."

She kept an eye on the guards who had run for ranged weapons as the two of them made their way to the back of the room and the large double doors which sealed them in.

A flash.

Ahrn screamed.

His body collapsed beside her, a deep smoking crater in his back exposing burned and blackened bone.

Bile rose in Senia's throat. Tears welling in her eyes.

"No!" she gasped, not enough breath for a scream.

Turning, she saw Prandol standing again, massaging his jaw, smiling grimly.

"Something tells me," he said, voice carrying, "he won't be going anywhere but straight to the Void."

The flames embracing Emberthorn turned blue.

This is new.

Senia felt only fire, pure rage, fill her.

Senia, what are you...? Are you well?

No.

Oh.

"Did I anger the little Scion?" the wizard taunted. Not a brilliant move on his part.

Two steps, then leaping with preternatural strength, she flew toward him.

A bright flash seared her eyes. Even blinded, she landed with grace, going to one knee as Emberthorn swept through empty space.

To the right!

Her hands pulled themselves and Emberthorn toward some attack she still couldn't see through the black haze over her sight. She sensed the light, the brilliant heat, and even felt the bolt of white-hot light where it hit Emberthorn's blade, blocked.

Ow! I had forgotten how much magic hurts.

Senia stood in one smooth movement, stalking toward the wizard, or at least where she thought he was. She tried to blink away the black spots obscuring her vision, but to no avail.

Where is he? Guide me.

To your left now, four more paces... oh?

What?

He just vanished.

"If light can't find me, then no one can see me. A neat little trick don't you think?"

The voice was to her left. She spun in with three quick steps, swinging Emberthorn's burning blade.

"Oh, close there, but not quite!"

It was instinct only that made her raise Emberthorn over her head, blade pointed down, guarding her back. As it was, the wizard's attack was only partially blocked by the move. Pain, hot and sharp, bit into her back, and she stumbled forward.

She was starting to regain her vision, but everything

was still blurry, and it seemed it wouldn't matter against this foe anyway.

She stopped, waiting, on guard, listening.

With the enhanced senses possessed while in contact with Emberthorn, she could hear the brush of the wizard's feet on the floor. This was her only recourse. She didn't know how to fight magic.

Anything you can do to help?

I... it's been so long since I've fought a true wizard with any power. I'm sorry Senia. Just listen.

So, she did.

The twang of a crossbow was keen in her ears, and her blade burned as it swept the speeding bolt from the air. In the next instant, the sizzle of heat warned her of another incoming bolt of light from the wizard, and she spun with the momentum of the heavy blade to block the magical attack.

Ah! That really hurts.

Sorry, but better you than me.

I suppose.

"Not bad, girl. I will admit I haven't had this much of a challenge in ages. You are everything my men have told me you'd be. But now it is time to die so I can take that little sword of yours to my master."

"I highly doubt that."

"You haven't even really touched me yet, what makes you think you have any chance against me? Just as your friend the monk fell to my magic, so shall you."

"I'm waiting."

"Wait no more."

A barrage of small beams of light streaked toward her.

Perfect. Just what she had hoped for.

She blocked all but one, which she spun away from. It put a hole in her blouse, singeing her side.

More came, as she had expected. She blocked, her blade moving faster than even she could imagine, moving in, stepping closer with each beam of light Emberthorn swept to the side.

She had him now.

Her sight might still be poor, but she could see where each beam was coming from, a single source, which was moving slowly to its right, trying to move away from where he had started the barrage at her.

She moved in, toward the original spot where he'd been, hoping he'd suspect his rouse was working.

Then, blocking three more beams meant to carve her into pieces, close now, she leapt towards him, slicing with the long reach of her blade through the space he should be.

He screamed.

Prandol became visible once more as he fell to the floor, left arm holding the stump of his shoulder where his right arm used to be. He knelt there for a moment, looking at her disbelieving before she removed his head as well.

She stood over him, breathing hard for a moment.

Another twang.

Her left hand caught the crossbow bolt an inch from her head, snapping it. Her speed and strength astonishing even her.

A deadly silence filled the room.

"Anyone else want to play?" In that moment, she wanted nothing more than to slay them all.

The Blacklord's men fled.

Her flaming anger faded.

The fire on Emberthorn went out.

Senia tossed the broken bolt aside and looked to where Ahrn lay. She rushed to him. Kneeling beside him, she was amazed to see his chest still rising, even if barely.

She laid a hand on his shoulder, and his one good eye fluttered open.

A pain wracked smile found his lips.

He was trying to speak.

She bent low.

"Hush, don't speak," she said, feeling how weak he was.

"I..." He winced in pain.

"Ahrn, no, please, don't..." *Don't speak, don't die, don't leave me, please just don't...*

"... L... Lo... love..." His eyes closed, his lips going slack.

His chest still rose, but each breath was ever so shallow.

Tell me there is something you can do for him!

I have no powers of healing.

Is there nothing at all you can do?

I...

Please! Hot tears streamed down her cheeks. *Please...*

I cannot heal, you need a Daughter of Ehlani or... I don't know, I'm sorry Senia.

That sparked an idea. *Wait! That's something. The monks, they know healing. They may be able to help him, but... but they're still a week away.*

I... There may be something I can do!

What? Please, quick. She was desperate, she'd take anything.

When I vanish, I go to a place with no time, nothing at all. I... I may be able to take him with me if I am touching him when you give the command. You won't have access to me if you want him to live, not for the week it takes to get to the monks, but he'll be as he is now when you get there.

I can do it, and... thank you. I know how much you hate that place.

You'll owe me for this.

I already owe you so much.

You'll owe me more.

I know.

She gently touched the flat of Emberthorn's blade to the back of Ahrn's leg and said, "Vanish."

Both of them were gone. She was left feeling weak and sick once again.

Suddenly, the burn on her back grabbed at her, pain throbbing through her. She gritted her teeth, forced herself to stand, and stumbled towards the open doors of the wizard's hall.

CHAPTER 13

Though her mind wavered, as unsteady as her body, she had sense enough to collect Ahrn's cloak and pack. She left hers behind. It held only clothes and a few sentimental items, his pack had all the supplies. Since they were of a height, his cloak fit her fairly well, and the addition of the hood would help to disguise her as well as provide added warmth during cool nights in the high hills.

She encountered no resistance leaving the keep and staggered out of the city as the dimness of twilight faded into full night. When she reached the top of the hill on which the city sat, twinkling lights below, she turned to see if there was any pursuit behind her.

Without her Scion abilities, it would be near impossible to tell, but her night vision had always been good, and she could see no one following her.

Exhausted, but unwilling to stop so close to the city, she lurched forward down the other side of the hill.

She walked through the night. Down one hill, forcing herself up the next. Clouds covered the light of the moon at some point, but she moved onwards. A light rain began, pattering on the oiled cloth of Ahrn's cloak.

Perhaps it was the rain's slow soaking or just her own senses returning to her, but she smelled him then. Ahrn's scent clung to the cloak, close around her, heavy and comforting. It gave her strength, and she pushed on through the night in the gathering rain.

The storm broke in full at dawn the next day, pouring water on her as she traversed a long ridge. Even with the gray gloom of the day clustered close to the ground, she could see the iron sides of Maalkin's Rise disappearing into the clouds far to her right.

She walked on, putting one foot in front of the other, her strides becoming short and weak until her legs began to ache, and she wanted nothing more than to rest. By this point, it was close to evening once again, the dark day fading to a darker night.

She found shelter under the boughs of a full and wide cedar. She huddled in her cloak on the bed of needles next to the trunk. Most of the rain cascaded outward over the clustered branches above. Dry for now, and warm enough, she fell asleep.

∼

She awoke to the crack of thunder as the storm intensified. She ate a few bites from the half loaf of bread and two strips of dried meat that remained of their food. It would have to last her a week. Her stomach growled and heaved, warily accepting the food despite the sting of her wounds and the disorientation pervading her mind and body with the separation from Emberthorn.

She had no idea how long she had slept, but it was day once again, if grim and dour, clouds clinging to the hills. Not even the mountains were visible.

The rain was even worse than before, and within an hour of leaving her shelter, she was soaked through.

Cold, tired, and hungry, she knew only that she needed to keep moving.

During one of their many discussions of what lay ahead, Ahrn had mentioned that past the hills there was a long valley with a forest. She knew she would be roughly on the right path as long as she wasn't heading higher up into the mountains.

When the storm scudded away at the end of the day, she could see the mountains still on her right, tall and stoic.

With the scent of him still clinging close, filling his cloak, she thought of Ahrn. Unbidden came the memory of the night, after their battle around the oak tree, when he had held her close, kissed her. She remembered what he had said with his final few breaths in the wizard's hall... 'love'. Could it truly be?

He'd been so distant after their kiss. Could he really feel as she felt?

Cresting a rise, she encountered a biting north wind, sucking the air and all other thoughts from her. She fled down the hill hoping to escape it, but it found her, funneling and blustering through the valley.

She found no shelter that night and simply tried to sleep on the cold earth under the open sky, but the wailing wind chilled her soaked clothes, and her teeth were chattering before long. She rose again, hoping movement would warm her. Legs weary, and ready to fail, she climbed yet another hill.

And another... and another...

Her thoughts became a torrent, whirling like the wind from one place to the next. From Emberthorn to Ahrn, her life before and the death she had dealt. Dark and light, night and day, all seemed blurred before her.

When next she came to herself, the sun was up, but the brutal wind had not let up. Between the sun and the wind, her cloak was mostly dry by midday, but when she removed it to let her shirt and skirt also dry, she found the wind too intense, shivering and trembling with the chill, feeling exposed, naked to its touch.

Instead, she found a small copse of trees, which sheltered her from the wind and provided enough dead branches to start a fire with Ahrn's flint and striker. She hung the cloak over the fire first, ensuring it was dry and warm, then stripped off her clothes, hanging them to hiss and steam in the rising smoke, huddled in the warmth of the cloak.

Night fell, and she ate another small supper. Too tired and worn to restrict herself, she ate all the meat and all but a small chunk of the bread before she realized what she had done. She ate the remaining bread, uncaring. Her thoughts were a shambles, as was her life, it seemed. She dressed again, clothes warm and smoky, but when she placed Ahrn's cloak around her once more, still heady with his scent it was too much for her. Despite the comfort of warm garments, she wept. All she loved had been taken from her, her family, a man she barely knew but who her soul cried out for, and her companion, her twin, her sword. She had nothing in this moment, empty and eternally alone. Finally, well past exhaustion, she fell asleep, rivulets of hot tears still wet on her cheeks.

~

*T*he howl of a wolf woke her.

It was the deep of night, and the sound had been close. Her fire was dead, and the wind still wailed amidst the hilltops. She rose quickly, gathered her things and, despite legs cramped with innumerable aches and a mind addled with grief, stumbled into the darkness.

For two more days, she staggered through the high hills, finding little shelter, little rest, and little comfort. It didn't rain again in the very least, but the wind remained cold and only served to seize up already sore muscles.

Her mind, like the wind, whirled and buffeted her with thoughts cold and dark.

She began to wonder, in the wavy state of near-delirium, if she hadn't turned herself around somewhere in the hills, and was heading off in the wrong direction, never to find this elusive abbey, never to find anyone, any comfort, and joy every again. Yet always she remembered Ahrn's words and kept the mountains to her right.

Finally, as evening closed on yet another day, she crested a hill but found this time, instead of more hills, a long valley stretching before her, swathed in a deep green blanket of forest.

That night she rested in the shelter of the trees, though she slept little. As the moon rose, she began to make her way through the forest, tripping and falling often. Her night vision, though still good, missed the occasional root. More often, it was simply her fatigue causing the missteps.

She came to a river and refilled her water skin which she'd drained the day before. Then, heedless of the icy waters, dipped her face in to drink. She stayed by that stream, even dozed a little as day broke. With fresh cold water splashed on her face and filling her stomach, she found a spark of energy and clarity then, deciding to follow the river through the valley for the rest of the day.

She emerged from the forest as the first stars twinkled to life in the night sky.

According to Ahrn, she would be in Hallania now. She was close, only a little farther, up some hills he had said.

The only hills before her were to her left, as a plain spread out before her on the right. She walked through the night, visions swimming before her eyes, Ahrn collapsing, the wizard falling before her, her family traveling long lonely roads. She imagined her parents, her true parents, long ago in some distant land fighting, dying, and in her fever of pain and sorrow, cursed them for leaving her.

Cursed everyone for leaving her, alone in a world of cold and pain.

Her legs trembled with every step, faltering more often than not. One hill she had to crawl to the top. Once there, she lay, breathing hard, her body throbbing, burning, muscles seized.

She forced herself onward, falling down the side of the hill, rolling, landing in a heap in the next valley. She wept, soul shattered, unable to move for the pain, hunger, and despair.

She slept there, uneasily, curled into a ball, and woke, so stiff and sore she could barely move.

Yet she stretched muscles that protested, crying out with each movement and the shock of pain it brought. She used the pain to waken her, move her, and found some reserve of strength to climb the next hill.

Cresting that hill, she saw a great fortress built on a high plain with walls taller than she would have thought possible. There were only two more rises between her and it.

She wept with joy for the sight and tried to run down the next hill, but her muscles would not abide, and again she tumbled down the sides, battered and further bruised. Yet this time she wasn't daunted. She rose despite the pain, the blood of a dozen cuts, the chill of the wind, and the ache in her soul.

Though she could only crawl, she clawed her way to the top of the next hill, found the wide dirt road which led to the abbey, and on hands and knees, forced herself up to its massive doors.

There she collapsed.

She heard the loud creak of the great doors opening. The footfalls of people running out, and with only one step left in her journey, she whispered, with a voice hoarse and dry. "Emberthorn."

There were gasps from around her.

She barely noticed as she slipped into the dark expanse of unconsciousness.

houghts and visions tumbled through darkness. Dreams livid and lurid danced in garish light and fire. Pain played and pressed, the wizard's fire touching her, the ache of being without Emberthorn, the soul-borne burn of leaving family and loving one who remained uncertain. Yet there was also joy in her bonding with Emberthorn, and the warmth of her feelings for Ahrn. All mixed and mingled in the fever and fire of her mind.

Then a voice.

Senia?

Emberthorn?

Hello, little one.

It was dark here. For a moment she thought perhaps she had joined Emberthorn in his 'nothing' space. *Where am I?*

St. Antin Abbey.

The abbey? She remembered the final moments, collapsing on the road. Yes, she had made it.

Why is it so dark?

You're still unconscious, you need to wake up.

Oh. Yet for the life of her, she didn't seem to know how.

I know what will get you up.

Yes?

Ahrn.

"Ahrn!" Light and breath flooded into her as she half rose on a soft pallet. She glanced around, gaining bearing quickly. Emberthorn was next to her on the small cot. Several candle-trees lit the room. Solid stone walls blocked in a small room, the bare bed, a small chest, a chamber pot and a single chair next to a small table crowded the space. The chair was occupied.

"Hello, young one." The speaker was an aging woman with steel-gray hair, a lined and weathered face, her look stern and solid. The woman was not large but exuded authority and confidence. Some distant remembrance pricked Senia's mind.

"I'm Master Elia." Senia smiled, recalling Ahrn's description of the woman and thinking it adequate.

"Ahrn will be happy you are alive. He was worried for you."

The woman raised a brow, a scant reaction. "Did he speak much of me?"

"Enough." She was unsure what to say to this woman. Senia adjusted herself, sitting cross-legged on the bed. She was wearing only a light shift, but the air in the room was warm and comfortable. She picked up Emberthorn, placing the sword on her lap, tracing the whorls and runes on the blade, comforted.

I'd missed that. Emberthorn purred.

Me too.

"It took two men to carry that sword in here and you pick it up like it was nothing." Senia looked up at the awe in the woman's voice. "I didn't believe, not truly, despite all evidence, not until now. A true blooded Guardian, here. It is a miracle."

Senia shook her head. "A miracle. I still cannot see it as such. This sword is a curse…"

Hey

Oh, shut up I'm just getting to the good part.

"…As much a blessing. I can't imagine being without it, but I honestly don't know what I will do with it. I was a simple girl in a simple village and now…?" She let the unsaid question hang.

"We will train you. The monks of Embreth know of all the Guardians and their Aehryn-Gifts. The Archives here are extensive and we will uncover all of your powers. We will help you become the Guardian you are meant to be."

But do I really want to be a Guardian?

Of course, you do.

Easy for you to say. You've always been one, I have always been a regular girl, a Guardian seems a lot to take on.

I'll help you.

I know, it's just…

Emberthorn was silent. She thanked him for it at this moment.

Senia smiled at Master Elia. "Ahrn believes in me,

perhaps that is enough." Her feelings all bubbled up then, affection and worry. She didn't know what had become of Ahrn, and now, suddenly, desperately needed to know. "How is he? Did he survive? He... We... I need to know... I need..." Words failed her as twin tears streaked down her cheeks. "Please tell me you were able to heal him."

Master Elia began to say something, stopped, her mouth closing. Her face became grave, still, solemn. She set her lips to speak once more but again paused, a heavy sigh leaving her. A sudden dark dread filled Senia.

"I'm sorry," Master Elia said, a hint of emotion breaking the stark facade. "We... could not."

"No!" And all the stones of the Abbey shook with the cry. Master Elia's stunned, surprised expression was the last Senia saw before tears filled her vision. She placed her head in her palms and wept, hot bitter rivers of sorrow. She couldn't hold herself up. She collapsed to her side on the cot.

As she did her world tilted also. Suddenly nothing was solid, everything shifted, slid from its moorings and plummeted into the abyss.

"I'm sorry." Master Elia's voice was close, a hand touched Senia's shoulder. "So... sorry, I... I'll leave you now. There are men outside your door if you require anything."

Soft footfalls barely audible above Senia's weeping, then the door opened and closed. Once again, with a finality Senia had never imagined, she was alone.

Something isn't right.

Senia was too lost in her emotions to answer, though

she'd heard the words. She knew very well that something wasn't right, her entire life wasn't right, not anymore.

Senia! Listen to me!

The shout jolted her. *What?* She wasn't in a mood to talk.

Senia, can't you feel that?

Feel what?

I'm not quite sure, but... I was connected to Ahrn for so long, together in that nothingness. I... I feel like I can still sense him.

What? Where? Senia didn't want to believe Emberthorn. For belief was hope, and she wasn't sure she could handle such an emotion if it weren't true.

I don't know, but can't you feel it? There is something, and... and I think it's you that's feeling it, not me. It's so small, so distant, it's hard to tell.

I can't... Emberthorn please, this is too much...

I'm sorry, my dear. Allow me to help. A warm wave of soothing peace spread into Senia. She drew a long shuddering breath, and her tears stopped.

Thank you.

She tried to steady herself, pushing herself up to sit once again. She closed her eyes and tried to focus.

Long deep breaths calmed her further, until finally... there was something.

What is that?

I don't know. It is familiar though, isn't it?

Very.

Do you think it could be...?

I... don't know, but I will find out.

She rose from her bed, bare feet brushing cool stone.

Emberthorn was in hand, her divining rod, trembling with the resonance of this deep, secret feeling shared between them.

She padded to the door, opened it, and moved through.

Two large monks stood on either side of the frame. They must have noticed the movement of the door since they turned to her. Both of them, upon seeing her, knelt with heads bowed.

"Mistress Scion," one said reverently. "How may we be of service?"

Uncertain, she paused for a moment before walking out between them.

"There is something I must do," she said, voice low.

"May we be of assistance?" one asked, standing.

She waved him back. "No, stay."

She didn't look, moving past, but knew they had complied, hearing the rustle of clothes as they resumed their post.

She glided down the long stone hall to the end where a thin, tall window allowed a strip of moonlight to illuminate the corridor.

Her senses were alive in the night. She felt the grain of the stone beneath her feet, though worn close to smooth by the passage of thousands of monks. Heard the barest creak of some monk adjusting his position in bed behind the door of the cell she passed. Inhaled the faint scent of roses, which grew stronger as she drew to the window.

The barest of breezes swept in, tousling hair and sleeping gown. Darkness hung beyond the window, a warm night. It would seem the chill north wind had faded, and summer was in the air.

She turned a corner, dark and abandoned. Few were up at this hour. Those who were she avoided easily as she moved along, hearing their approach down halls long before they would have noticed her. She became twin to silence and darkness. This was a quest for her alone, following a distant call only she could hear.

She found stairs, descended, and moved along many corridors past so many identical doors. How she knew which one drew her, she was unsure, except that her heart sung at the nearness of her goal.

There... a door. Reverently she placed her soft hand on the course wood and knew, without a doubt that what pulled her lay beyond this threshold.

There were voices within.

CHAPTER 15

*A*hrn still marveled at his life, his health, his wholeness.

Sitting on the edge of his cot, he ran his hands over what had been burned flesh, finding only smooth skin. His back, the side of his head, his ear, his hair, all were perfect, unharmed, whole.

No pain.

"High Sister Olinda does know her trade," Master Elia said. "Though you'll have to thank all the Gods, especially Reisha of the Fates, for the luck that brought that small group of Daughters of Ehlani within our walls not but a week before you arrived. Without them, you may have lived, but you would not be whole. Only the Daughters know the magic of stitching muscle and bone, flesh and hair, back together."

Ahrn looked up at the second miracle of the day.

"And you. I had hoped you had survived the assassins, but I was never certain."

"It will take more than that to finish this old hag."

Ahrn smiled.

He had awoken only a few hours past, finding himself whole, hearty and with a raging appetite. Monks had brought food, but he had been told to stay in his cell until the Master and the High Sister could check in on him. High Sister Olinda had come first, checking his wounds and clucking on about his swift recovery, telling him to eat well for the next few days to replenish his body. Not long after Master Elia had arrived, alive and well.

"I'm glad you are well." Though even as he spoke the words another thought entered his head, one that had been nagging him from the moment he woke. "Is Senia well?"

"Senia? Is that the name of the miracle of a girl that brought you here, the Scion?"

"Yes." And Ahrn couldn't help but think that 'miracle' was exactly the right word for her.

Something crossed Master Elia's face, some hidden thought. "Yes." The word was drawn out, tentative. "We need to speak of her."

"She is amazing." A memory rushed back to him. It was hazy, clouded by pain, and his want at the time to slip away to the void where pain could not touch him. He had told Senia, said the words that were in his heart. He had thought he would die and no longer needed to hide anything.

Yet, what now?

"I love her, Master Elia."

There was no answer.

Looking back to Master Elia, she was looking at him keenly, eyes sad. She shook her head slowly. "No Ahrn, you don't."

He met her gaze, intent, true. "I do, but I don't know what to do about it."

"Don't say this. You're a hero, Ahrn. You've found what we had thought lost. There is perhaps hope for our fight against The Blacklord. But you know that you cannot be with her, you know our vows forbid it." She rose, head still shaking, and came to kneel beside his bed. She took his hand in hers, rough, calloused, aged. "Forget what you have said, it is probably just her aura as a Scion. You are enchanted, a youthful infatuation, that is all, but do not say that you love her."

He looked away. How could he deny the truth? Could she not see that he had to be honest with himself? He knew now, having come so very close to death, that he could no longer deny his love. He wanted to be with Senia, forever, hold her, have her, be there for every moment in her life. Was that not love?

"I cannot ignore my heart."

She squeezed his hand hard, and he looked back to her. Her eyes captured his, searching. She stayed like that for some time, her voice was low when she spoke. "Yes, I can see that."

He squeezed her hand back, his sincerity firm in every word. "I was dead. As close to death as one can be and still live. I have seen the depths of my own heart. I cannot hide what I feel anymore. I may be breaking every vow to our God, but somehow, I cannot bring myself to believe that she would keep me from such a desire as this. What I feel is true and is that not what Embreth is at her core, truth? If I deny this truth, then I am no monk of hers."

"You will be the downfall of us all, boy." But the tone wasn't harsh. She shook her head. Ahrn raised a brow in question. Her response was measured, she weighed every word as a miser does gold.

"There is a teaching of Embreth. It is something only the masters know, and it is never shared with anyone who hasn't reached that level of ability. I trust you with this Ahrn, as a dedicated student of Embreth. I hope I'm not mistaken. This teaching is simple. It states that, of everything Embreth stands for, Truth, as you say, is above all. There can be no love above our love for her and for Truth. No love... but one. No love but... True Love."

Ahrn's heart flooded with relief. Perhaps all would not be lost for his love!

"Master Elia, I..." She cut him off.

"There is a reason we do not share this teaching Ahrn. There are many out there who wouldn't be able to tell the wings of infatuation from the solid depths of true love. We have always been concerned that our monks would think themselves to be in a 'true love', when in fact they are not."

She looked into his eyes, his soul once again. "I can see your love and it is pure, true." Master Elia looked away, eyes closed, letting out a long heavy sigh. "I just hope it doesn't destroy us all."

"What? How?"

"If you are seen to be in love then..."

He found her thought and finished it. "Then others will want to know how this can be."

"Yes. Either our secret must come out, or you will be banished. Yet I fear that if this girl feels for you as you do for her then banishing you will only harm her deeply, weakening the one weapon we have against The Blacklord."

Ahrn remained silent. Only now did her exact words from earlier ring true to him: 'don't say this' not, 'you cannot feel this'. It had been a warning, a hint. If he kept his mouth shut about his feelings, did not speak of them, then no one need know. Yet they both knew he wouldn't be able to remain silent.

"I fear I have made a grave mistake." Her words were careful, measured. "I couldn't have known your love was true. Ahrn, I spoke with Senia just now, I told her... I told her you were dead."

"What?" Ahrn suddenly recalled how distant Senia had been in those many days before the Wizard. He wondered, briefly, did she weep for his loss, or did she even notice. "What did she do?"

"She broke... and the stones of the abbey trembled with her cry." Master Elia sighed, and when she spoke next her tone was odd, as if she were trying to convince herself now, not him. "But there are so many reasons you cannot be together. It will distract her from her training. It will throw our order into chaos. Ahrn, I was sure that this relationship could not be, that it would not last. A Scion is for all people, and there will be many who need her, who seek her attentions. Many calls she will not be able to ignore. I was certain that my decision was right, to cut the connection between you and she before it could become... what it already is.

His heart fell.

"I had thought," she continued, "to convince you to leave before she discovered the ruse. I had hoped you would honor your vows, that you felt not love, but only affection. I see now that won't be an option. You won't leave her, will you?"

"No." His voice was solid, strong. "I will never leave her."

Master Elia nodded with a sigh. "Then I guess it is time for all secrets to be revealed. The monks of Embreth must know of this higher law." She released his hand and rose. A faint smile found her lips. "I always knew you would be trouble."

He returned the smile. His heart finally at ease.

The door to his cell opened. There framed in the entrance was Senia, tall beautiful, radiant, Emberthorn held distractedly in one hand.

"I knew it could not be," she said, her voice holding within the heavy burden of a hope held tightly, now finally realized.

"I think I'll leave you two alone." Master Elia said, moving toward the door. "That is if the Scion can forgive me and has mercy enough to let me live?"

Senia glanced at Master Elia, a shadow of ire and grief passing over her features before she waved dismissively. "He is alive, that is all I care about."

CHAPTER 16

*M*aster Elia left. Senia stepped into the room. Ahrn sat on his cot, looking lovingly at her, golden eyes catching the light from the tree of candles on the small table in the corner.

She closed the door behind her.

This was a dream.

It had to be a dream, for only in her dreams was Ahrn alive and unharmed, as he had been before the wizard had scorched him. A smile grew on his face of purest joy and desire. He had never before worn such an expression for her. This must be a dream.

Yet she knew this was real. She had heard what had passed between the two within the room as she listened outside. Ahrn had been healed by Daughters of Ehlani, but more wondrous than that... he loved her!

If you're about to do what I think you're about to do, I think I'll only be in the way...

Her thoughts were barely on Emberthorn, but he had a

point. "Float." She recalled he had mentioned the command so very long ago. Releasing the blade, Emberthorn hung in the air. She lightly pushed the sword aside, sending it hovering into a corner of the room.

Ahrn blinked. "What...?"

"It doesn't matter, not now. I'll tell you later."

Rising from the bed, heedless he came to her, strong arms around her, crushing her in an embrace. His touch became the key to her soul, soothing all worries and unlocking all her vast reserve of passion and longing. Her arms wrapped around him, tight, her cheek to his, the softness of her body tight against the harness of his.

Her emotions flamed and billowed within her, filling her every pore and every fiber of every muscle.

"You're alive," she breathed, so grateful for that one simple truth.

He released her just enough to bring his face before hers, tears in his eyes. He spoke, his voice hoarse, soft yet heavy with emotion. "I thought I would never see you again, and here you are. You're truly are a miracle. I love you Senia, and I shall until I die... again." The last he added with a hint of a laugh.

Before she could answer his lips found hers, and he tightened his embrace once again. His kiss was hard, intense.

Not a dream, but better, more than she could have ever envisioned. All her desires were being fulfilled. Dream or no, she would let herself float in the wonder of this singular moment.

His eyes opened, surprised as she pushed into his kiss, tongues touching.

Her body, already made sensitive from her connection with Emberthorn, tingled with heightened awareness. She could feel the coarse cloth of his monk's attire through the thin fabric of her shift, and every slip of friction between them burned with bliss.

Her hands slipped under his shirt, finding cool skin over hard muscles.

"By the Gods, your hands... are hot!"

She couldn't even respond, the air sucked from her voice by the flames in her chest. She ran her hands up his body, over the rolling hills of his abdomen, to a wide hard chest, and thick round shoulders. His shirt was up around his chin now, and she simply continued to explore the chill of his skin up his hard, round arms as she removed it entirely. When her hands met his, high over their heads, his fingers curled around hers, holding them tight, and he leaned in for another long and luxurious kiss.

This time as his naked chest, hard and cool as stone, pressed against the sheer fabric of her shift, she simply let herself go. Diving fully into the burning emotions within her.

She stood before him, her body trembling. She cupped his face in her hands and chocked out the words which were lodged in her heart.

"I love you Ahrn."

Then she put her hands on his shoulders and pushed him back the two steps, so his legs were against his bunk.

Taking a step back with a single fluid motion, she removed her shift and stood before him exposed.

This time, unlike when he'd seen her in bathing in the river, he reacted. Removing his breeches, he came to her, scooping her up in strong arms and indulging in a passionate kiss before setting her on the bed.

Then there was only passion... two bodies merged as one.

CHAPTER 17

Senia stood atop the high ramparts of St. Antin Abbey in the new light of dawn. The warm south wind streamed her hair to the side, wild and free, wisps tickling across her face.

Ahrn was next to her, strong arms around her, comforting.

It had been a week since her night with Ahrn.

The next day Master Elia and the Other Masters of the Order of Embreth had told the monks of the Higher Law. It was new and fresh, some still unsure, but Senia and Ahrn were not going to hide their love. Standing atop the fifty-foot walls they were a beacon of love to all who saw them.

Yet darker tidings threatened to overshadow their fledgling relationship.

Senia watched as a long line of men, horses, wagons, weapons, and wounded wove their way up the hills and through the gates of the Abbey.

Kingdoms were falling to The Blacklord's armies. She

had known so little, living in her little village, unaware that for years The Blacklord had been storming ever closer. Many wars had been fought in the east to keep The Blacklord at bay. She had learned a lot in her week at St. Antin. First Thania fell, fifteen years hence, then Perolia not five years ago. Now Vohria was taken as well. This meant The Blacklord's realm now stretched as far west as the Velanor River, a great and wide divide between kingdoms. Yet if rumors were to be believed, The Blacklord's armies had crossed the Velanor, and Sandria in the south, once Ahrn's home, was now taken. Also, Aestria, Senia's home until just a few weeks ago, was waging a losing war, and the armies fleeing to the Abbey at the moment were what remained of the Hallanian forces that had tried to block The Blacklord's advance into their kingdom.

For two, in such a large world, love had prevailed. But peace was still a far-flung dream. Senia knew that if she were to be the hero that these kingdoms needed her to be, she needed to fully embrace and uncover all of her Scion abilities.

Monks waited for her in the large yard of the abbey below. She was to train with them, learn the full extent of her martial prowess and the powers of Emberthorn.

You've changed, Emberthorn remarked idly.

I'm not the girl I was when I left Alindale. It was a fact, no regrets.

No, no you aren't. You feel... harder.

A good word. It seems an eternity since I left home. Dragged through the dregs of the Deepest Void, then, finally shown the brilliance of the Heavens. Yet even that seems overshadowed now.

A long road. Longer still to come I think. A great sigh.

What?

It's silly.

She laughed at that. *What is it Em?*

She sensed a smile, a pause. *It's just... well... I kind of liked that innocent girl.*

You're a weapon. A tool of war and death, you can't expect me to stay innocent for long around you, can you?

No, but... it was nice, for a while, to have someone who was so... open, so young and fresh as my companion. Truly pure of heart.

She grimaced at his choice of words. 'Pure' was a word that had been floating through her thoughts. She and Ahrn had shared a bed since that night a week ago. *You're referring to what happened between Ahrn and I?*

No. As much as I didn't want any part of that, it was pure, in its own way. Your soul is pure, but your heart... It's hard. All the death and loss, which I know is because of me, well, you just don't look at the world the same way.

No. I don't. It used to be full of light and laughter. Now... Looking out at the line of weary men headed to the abbey and, in the distance, a great black pall hanging over the land... *I see only darkness ahead.*

Exactly.

I don't think that's going to change anytime soon.

No, I guess not.

Time to train then. I will become the weapon the world needs me to be.

Ahrn looked over at her, and she realized she had said that last bit out loud.

"If you are a weapon, you are a weapon of peace, of love and purity. Never forget that," he said, his voice soft. He smiled at her. She knew he couldn't see the hardness within her. In his eyes, she was still Senia, soft and innocent.

And that was one of the reasons she loved him.

Kissing him, long and lingering, arms entwined, she felt the darkness within diminish.

She grinned as they separated. "Race you down."

He rolled his eyes, knowing he couldn't win.

She took five long strides to the other side of the thick wall, then off.

Air rushed around her as she felt strength far beyond normal swell in her legs. She landed lightly with a slight spring, not the least fazed by the fifty-foot drop and walked into the swarm of monks waiting to train her.

SCION RISING
The Guardians Of Light: Book 2

He'd have to be crazy to follow her.

Wyllea is certain she's going mad, or at least as certain as an insane person might be. The voice in her head is not her own and it's been getting stronger as she grows weaker, trapped without provisions behind enemy lines. She needs help... soon, before she loses herself entirely. But the only man she can trust is a thief and rogue.

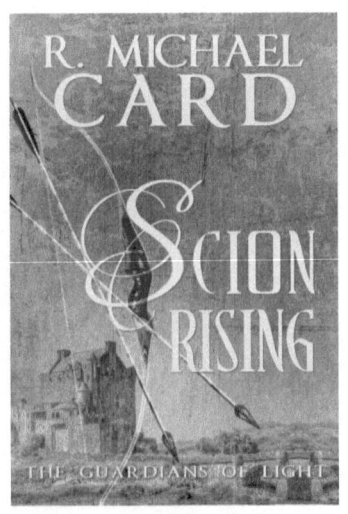

Tirol just wants to be free and left alone, but he's been living in a land occupied by the Blacklord's army, dodging their "recruiters" for months in the wasted lands of the east. Then the mysterious Wyllea walks into his life asking for his help and he finds he can't refuse her. As much as he wants to avoid any sort of entanglement and simply walk away, he helps her, as crazy as she and her quest might be.

PROLOGUE

The night sang a discordant chorus of battle and Senia danced wildly to the tune.

The armies of The Blacklord had come to St. Antin Abbey. Within that fortress, the monks of Embreth and what remained of the forces of Hallania stood against them. The Blacklord's men outnumbered the allies by over twenty to one. The allied forces, however, had the strong walls of the abbey to guard them and a fully trained scion to defend them. All told, it was an even fight.

Senia leapt. Her massive sword, Emberthorn, blazed with living fire in her hands. From a distance, she might have seemed like a spark flashing up from the combat on the hills before the abbey. Hundreds of feet up and across, she sailed through the air, lazily flipping herself backward. She landed lightly, elegantly, on the fifty-foot wall of the abbey next to Ahrn.

Her lover used all of his fighting prowess to fling The Blacklord's magically enhanced, black-clad assassins off the wall. The assassins led the fight, jumping to the top of the walls and trying to clear a path for the hundreds of regular warriors with ropes and ladders waiting below.

A lull of battle around them gave enough time for her to lean in for a short but passionate kiss. She disengaged with a grin.

"How are the defenses?"

"Well enough. Two forces topped the wall in the past hour, but we rebuffed both."

"Keep up the good work."

"If you're heading out again, there's a Fire Wizard on that hill," He pointed, "who's been giving us some trouble."

Senia saw a stream of fire blowing from the hill in question to the top of the walls not far away.

"I'll give him some trouble then." Another grin and she was off, bounding from the wall, arching high over the battle to land on the hilltop.

The wizard, a woman, started at the sudden arrival of Senia before her. That hesitation was enough of an opportunity for Senia to spin in and slice her in twain, eliminating that threat.

For a moment, there was peace around her. The battle raged below her as The Blacklord's men surged forward around the hill she stood upon, but there were no threats here.

The allies held, but these nightly attacks wore away at the defenses and the hope of those within the abbey. Runners had been sent west to the nations of Fjoria, Scandia, and Nehrista, kingdoms to the west. Help had been promised, but it had yet to arrive. Senia feared without that help, despite her best efforts, The Blacklord's armies would probably overtake the walls of the abbey sometime before the end of the summer. She was doing her best, but they simply had far too many of the magical assassins and wizards for her to deal with, and more arrived daily.

She sighed and turned to leap back into the fray, but something stopped her.

It was an odd sensation, something she couldn't name.

She connected to the essence, the presence within her sword. *Emberthorn, what is that?*

I... it's been so long I can't be sure, but... Emberthorn's usually sure and steady baritone, which spoke within her mind, was hesitant.

But what?

There's an ability the monks mentioned in your training, one which they didn't talk much about as they figured it would never be used.

Senia racked her brain to remember, but the memory eluded her. *I...*

You have the ability to sense other scions, but I... I never thought... And this doesn't feel quite right either. It's been a while, but I'm sure I've never felt a scion that felt quite so...

Dark.

Yes.

Can you locate them?

I... yes. Actually... they're headed this way.

Indeed, the sensation, the pull, she felt toward this unknown source was moving, drawing nearer...

A moment later, descending from the night sky, a form landed on the hilltop near her, a tall, looming figure.

"Hello, Senia." His deep, resonant bass carried easily on the whispered breeze of the night. She didn't recognize the voice, nor what she could make out of him. He was quite tall, though his body was well proportioned so he did not seem 'lanky' as some taller men did . He was actually very well built, with thick, rolling muscles under his black shirt that accentuated his broad shoulders and wide chest. The fabric of his sleeves pulled tight over great, round biceps and forearms. Moonlight caught his features: sharp nose, heavy brow, rigid lines, strong jaw, framed by thick and full dark hair. He wore a smile that sent a chill down her spine. There was something about him that drew her, caught her and held her, yet another force equally as strong that scared her, shook her.

"Do I know you?" she said, wary. Though still there was a tingling within her that she somehow knew or should trust this man.

"You will, soon enough."

"Who are you?" she breathed.

"You can call me Davar." Several strides of his long legs brought him to within a sword's length distance. He looked her over, appraising. The gaze from those cold eyes enveloped her, powerful and dominating.

"What are you?" Senia asked.

"I've been sent to fetch you, bring you back... into the fold."

"Are there other scions?"

A pause. "Yes. Come with me and I'll show you."

No, don't.

I know he's lying, but how do I know? Why do I feel so sure I should trust this man and yet still somehow know he's lying?

I don't know.

"Perhaps," she said diplomatically. "At the moment however, I have a war to fight. Care to join me?"

He sighed, heaving round shoulders, eyes dark, piercing. "I didn't really think the ruse would work. If you can feel me the way I can feel you, then you already know—" He stopped himself short, as if coming too close to a flame. His next words were a mere breath, whispered. "Amazing. Such a shame."

With lightning speed, he reached back over his shoulder and drew a long dark blade that drank in the light around it and lunged at her.

She raised Emberthorn, blocking the strike, knocking it to the side. Yet the man's strength and speed were incredible. She had barely kept him from skewering her. Even now, in the blink of an eye before his next move, his blade hovered dangerously close to her side. She had only just managed to move it out of the way. The resistance against Emberthorn was immense. If this man wasn't a scion, he was certainly something she had never faced before.

He took a step back. His eyes ranged over her, measuring her.

She also stepped away, readying Emberthorn.

His blade was shorter, the length of a long broadsword, what some of the mercenaries called a hand-and-a-half sword or bastard sword. He held it easily in his left hand. She had the advantage when it came to blade length, but she had a sneaking suspicion he had the advantage when it came to knowing his opponent. He knew her, somehow, but she knew nothing of him or his capabilities.

You have no idea who this is? Why he's attacking me? She asked Emberthorn.

No, I'm just as confused as you. He is a scion... I think, but... Not.

I've never felt anything like him before.

Great.

He came in again, though it was clear within these first few strikes that he was testing her and the range of her weapon. He backed off again.

"Why are you doing this? Who are you?" she asked.

"I do what I must."

She had no idea what that meant. Her confusion was becoming a growing thread of fear. She did not like the power she sensed in this man.

He attacked in earnest.

His blade, swallowing light and dimming the area around them, was barely visible against the night, even more so for the speed with which he wielded it.

For a moment, she was on the defensive blocking his attacks. He was good, terrifyingly so. He was pushing her back, step by step. Since she'd bonded with Emberthorn no other man had ever felt a true threat, too slow, too weak, but Davar was... something else entirely.

She leapt, flipping back and away. In the air, she spotted a copse of trees behind her on the hilltop. A long branch reached out from one tree, and she landed on it, balancing easily.

"I warn you—" Her fear grew, and she needed time to

collect herself, but the rest of her words were cut off as he came flying at her in a leap of his own. Then they were both on the branch, engaged again, blades trimming the trees around them.

Davar knelt suddenly, shearing easily through the branch they stood on. Senia had been on the outer end and it fell from under her. She strengthened her legs and landed on her feet, but he was jumping down, blade slicing through the night. She blocked, but he feinted, moving his blade around hers, catching her on her left arm, cutting a shallow gash. The shock of someone actually landing a blow on her rang through Senia and Emberthorn.

This was wrong, so very wrong. She staggered away, swiping Emberthorn in front of her to back him off, but he leapt over the blade, striking down on her again. Senia, stunned by this move, failed to block, managing only to flinch to the side. His blade scored again, a light strike on her cheek, then a deeper cut across her upper chest and the bicep of her right arm.

Emberthorn's instincts took over, controlling her body, and she lashed out. But Davar's dark blade stopped the attack meant to shear him in two across his upper torso. It almost seemed as if it had been easy for him to block her heavier blade.

They stood there for a moment, close, her blade on his as she strained to end him. He simply smiled at her as he held Emberthorn at bay.

"They told me you would be harder than this." He didn't laugh, but there was mirth in his eyes. He was moving again, ducking under her blade, forcing it past him, then striking quickly at her thigh. Another hit, this one deep, the pain searing into her. Emberthorn's blazing spirit filled her with strength, keeping her upright, barely.

She was truly scared now, and a terror-born rage was burning within her. The flames licking along Emberthorn's blade turned a blazing blue as she retaliated. She attacked furiously, a blur of azure in the night. Davar was forced back, blocking and evading.

She used her reach advantage to keep him at bay, striking quickly yet keeping herself out of range. Finally, he leapt back, flinging himself to the far side of the hilltop. She hurled herself after him. She had the advantage, and she wouldn't give it away, nor would her fury allow him to escape, not now.

She descended upon him, Emberthorn slashing down, blue flames streaming in the dark. He blocked the blow, but the force of it sent him to one knee. He rolled away, coming to his feet with a quick and easy grace.

By all the gods! Was this what it was like to fight against her?

No, most people who fight you go down much easier. Emberthorn chimed in.

Ah.

She charged in.

He was set and ready, the expression on his chiseled features grim, dark.

She set upon him with all the skill and precision that her bond with Emberthorn and the past months of training allowed her. He backed up steadily now, blocking her blows, though she did score a hit to his forearm and another across his ribs.

She knew she had him, his blade was slowing. He had to be tiring. She lunged—

But he wasn't there.

It had been a lure, but she saw it far too late. He evaded the lunge, stepping to the side. He'd been backed up against a large tree and her blade slid easily through the thick trunk. She would have been able to withdraw it easily, given the heartbeat it would take to do so, but he didn't give her the time.

His blade came down onto her wrists. She saw the attack coming and barely had time to release Emberthorn and withdraw her hands... but that was a mistake she couldn't afford.

She'd been bonded with Emberthorn long enough that she retained much of her powers when not in contact with him, but she was still slower, if only a fraction. That was all he needed.

Even in the time it took her to say "Embertho—" to call the sword back to her hands, he spun and struck the flat of his blade hard against the side of her head.

She went down, vision blurring, the soft long grasses cushioning her little as she crashed to the ground.

"Ember..." She tried once again, but he struck her hard on the back of her head and her world spun into darkness.

CHAPTER 1

*W*yllea was sure she was going mad.

She'd seen her entire company slaughtered and was the only survivor. She'd been stranded behind enemy lines for nearly two months. She'd had one scant meal in the past three days and though she'd been able to find fresh water often enough, she was sure she would soon die from lack of food. And before she died, her mind would play tricks on her as it was now.

I'm not your mind playing tricks. I'm real.

She was sure that's what all the voices in crazy people's heads said. The trouble was she'd actually started responding to the voice. It had been getting stronger and stronger, harder to resist, over these past weeks as she'd tried to survive in a dark and barren land.

You're real? Not some figment of my imagination?

As real as the bow in your hand.

That's going a little far don't you think?

No, because I AM the bow in your hand.

You are the bow? I'm talking to a bow, a weapon. I'm talking to a bow inside my own head.

Yup, she was going crazy.

The other odd thing about the voice was... it wasn't any voice she recognized. She would have thought if she were creating some fantasy "self" to talk to in her head it would respond in her own voice or maybe that of her mother or someone she had known, but this voice she couldn't place. It was a woman's voice, strong and sure, low and resonant. She'd never heard any voice like it.

Wyllea, you are not going crazy! You must listen to me. I can help get us out of this mess!

Sure.

I can, if you'd just let me in.

Let you in? Aren't you already in? You've been bugging me for weeks now. I'd say that's pretty well in, don't you think?

No, I'm not. I'm in your head, yes, but that's not the same. Besides, it's taken me years of being by your side and then these past few weeks of your mind and body being so weak and strained that your natural defenses are down for me to speak to you this clearly. You need to let me in all the way, believe in me, who I am, what I can do. You need to bond with me.

Bond with you?

Really? This was where her crazy was taking her? Bonding to a voice in her head. She'd never been one for marriage, having spent her life as a mercenary. She'd had her fair share of men, some of whom she might have even considered laying aside her bow and settling down with if they'd ever wanted such things. But she'd never considered being with a woman, let alone bonding with one.

Especially if that woman was herself. That was just... crazy. Well, that explained it then.

Wyllea, please listen to me. I don't even know if it's possible, but I think it may be. I've never been able to speak to anyone like this before, not since my Guardian died and all of his line with him. I think perhaps...

Shut up, bow.

My name is Eaglewing.

Really? That's the name I've come up with for the voice in my head?

No, that's the name that was given to the bow in your hand. You've seen the images traced on it, the eagle in flight. That's me.

That's very logical of you, Eaglewing. In fact, I'm sure I've seen all those tracings. And perhaps with this bow being all I have left in the world I've seen them far too much lately, which is why I've associated the voice in my head to my bow. Yes, that makes sense.

Now you're the one talking crazy.

I'm pretty sure we're both crazy, actually.

Wyllea, please!

Shhh! Did you hear that?

What? Oh, yes. Sorry, you were distracting me. It sounds like... a hammer... hitting an anvil.

How would you know?

I've been around.

I'm not quite sure what that means. Now shut up, Eaglewing, and let me see what's going on.

Fine, but I'll be back. I'm not giving up on this.

I'm sure. Now, now shut up!

Wyllea was in a barren land and hadn't seen a village

in weeks. The Blacklord's men had pillaged and plundered these lands over a year ago. Crops reaped early to feed tens of thousands of men had had no one to replant them as the people here had also been taken. All that remained were fallow fields, black earth, and scavengers. Wyllea had kept herself close to water, knowing that much of survival, following a small river north and west toward Maalkin's Rise. She'd heard there were still those resisting The Blacklord in Hallania, north of the mountains, and hoped to join with them if she could slip past the front lines. On a clear day, she could see the mountains jutting up, gray and stark, to the north and west. She was fairly certain she was now in the land which had once been Vohria, but that still meant hundreds of miles to go to reach Hallania.

She was unsure she'd make it that far. She knew little of hunting. True, her aim with a bow was second to none; there simply wasn't any game to shoot. Three weeks ago she'd found a small refugee camp that had shared some food, but those were the last people she'd seen. With no easy food and no people to help her, she was going to die out here, alone. If there was a forge ahead, as the noise she'd heard suggested, that meant people and possibly help.

She'd been in a hillier land these last few days and there was a hill in front of her blocking her from seeing the true source of the noise. She crept up the hillside to peer over the top.

In the next valley was a small village. It sat on an east-west road, well paved and wide, which cut through the hills. There was a bridge over the river as well. She could see why The Blacklord's armies might keep this little village intact as a rest stop for messengers heading back to The Blacklord's realm or new recruits being sent to the front.

The sound she'd heard emanated from a squat building on the south side of the road with thick black smoke billowing from its chimney. A smithy would be another reason to keep the town intact. Not only was it a rest stop, but a place to fix weapons and armor, shoe horses, or make whatever other metalwork the army might need.

This brought up a very simple question for Wyllea, yet one very hard to answer: Should she go down to the village or avoid it?

Every fiber of her being said to avoid it. Every fiber that is, except her stomach.

"Maybe if I have a decent meal the voice will go away."

Don't count on it.

Shut up!

Eaglewing didn't reply, though strangely Wyllea got the vague impression of a sigh and a slow shake of the head.

This was really going too far. She needed a meal. She could risk the village... she hoped.

ABOUT R. MICHAEL CARD

R. Michael Card has loved fantasy since he read his first Dragon Lance book so many years ago. He has been writing for twenty years, but has only recently decided to start sharing his work with the world. He has always enjoyed the lighter side of epic fantasy, the grand adventure, and has infused that love into his works.

He lives near Toronto Ontario with his beloved wife and their cat. He has had a plethora of careers, working in software, insurance, trades, and education, with jobs ranging from washing cars to career counseling.

www.ingramcontent.com/pod-product-compliance
Lightning Source LLC
Chambersburg PA
CBHW030614130626
46552CB00002B/563